Aeolus Still Whispers

Cymen Van Arme

Published by New Generation Publishing in 2021

First Edition

ISBN

	Paperback	978-1-80369-003-2
	Hardback	978-1-80369-004-9

www.newgeneration-publishing.com

 New Generation Publishing

Saudade: Portuguese origin. A love that remains after someone special is gone.

It can also be the recollection of feelings, experiences, places or even events that once brought excitement, pleasure, well-being, which now activates the senses and makes one live again, or not, as many a case may be, as it describes a deep nostalgic longing.

In this emotion, there is a repressed knowledge that what one is longing for will never return. It can be described as a vast void, and it could be your children, friends or a thing you used to do when very young that should be there in a particular moment that is now missing.

But with love, it goes deeper. Indeed, into the abyss. A special person. The love of your life who has gone forever.

Chapter One

A drop of Nelson's blood?

In the late summer of 1971, a young boy, Gideon, was in the bar of a wonderfully seedy and dated Art Deco style hotel in Valletta, Malta, with slow-moving ceiling fans, potted palms and an African theme throughout. He was overwhelmed by the genuine 1920s décor.

He marvelled at the sounds and Mediterranean smells of the building with all its faded beauty. He had never been in a scene like this in his life. It was like being on a movie set with all the strange and exotic people meandering around – were they all planning Machiavellian tactics to thwart the good guys? Well, he sincerely hoped so.

The boy was a lowly but honourable Ordinary Seaman serving on his first ship, HMS Euryalus, a Leander Class Frigate of the Royal Navy. It was berthed alongside the old bastioned Fort of St Angelo in Grand Harbour, garrisoned by the British in 1800 and eventually re-commissioned as HMS St Angelo in 1933 as the headquarters for the Mediterranean fleet. It was now being used as the spearhead for the withdrawal of British service personnel from the island.

Gideon was just seventeen years and five months old.

With him was his much older friend and mentor, Mickey, a hard-bitten, long-serving Londoner with a rakish grin and a rolling gait, who was a Leading Seaman. He had accompanied Gideon so as to not arouse the suspicion of their superiors over a clandestine meeting.

They were in that hotel to meet a sophisticated thirty-four-year-old Greek woman. Mickey and Gideon were having a beer at that bar when a glamorous, slender woman walked into that room and the boys' whole world went into slow motion.

Dark and exotic and standing at five foot nine inches tall, with an abundance of luxuriant, jet-black shiny hair cascading over her left shoulder, she had an hourglass figure and her complexion had a flawless olive hue. This was made more evident by her fashionable Italian white cotton dress in a 1940s style, which made her look like a moving sculpture. A sculptor could not have fashioned this seraph's ears and Grecian nose any more seductively.

She smiled as she spotted the young boy and his mentor, and everybody had stopped talking just to look at her as she seemingly glided across the floor. Her muscle definition was perfect and she moved with the confidence of peak fitness, radiating what Mickey had once called an 'intelligent beauty.' Gideon sort of understood, without understanding. But he had known this lady for some weeks now, so he knew that she was endearingly unaware of just how alluring, elegant and lovely she was.

She commanded the full attention of everyone in the bar and yet her eyes were solely on him as she walked towards the two of them. She stopped in front of Gideon and kissed him softly on the lips, which sent an electric shock through his whole body, whilst her fingers gently caressed his neck and her thumb stroked the small, soft place in front of his ear. Her touch incapacitated him. Her eyes were black as obsidian with flecks of blue, and sparkled like jewels in her angelic face. They might have been truth-enhancing, with a shield against negativity just like the legend she had told him about one balmy evening by a moon-drenched, placid pool.

"Gordon Bennett Ma'am," said Mickey. "You look fuckin' – I mean bleedin' lovely today, like an angel."

She bowed slightly and smiled as she lightly touched his arm. "Thank you for all your loyalty and discretion, Michael."

He stood there for some seconds before the penny dropped that his services were no longer required. Then he downed his drink. "Right, I have your back, Ma'am and you… you little shit," he said to the boy, "I'll see you later down the Gut for some of Nelson's blood." And off he went into the dusty, chaotic streets of the city, probably to fend off dastardly boarders and to tell outrageous tales of sighting mermaids from oceans afar.

"What a perfectly charming character and a fine example of a man's man. He's a diamond in the rough, but a good guy, undeniably," said the Greek woman, whose name was Xanthe. They sat down in a covert alcove, where they could see the whole bar and yet few could see them, snuggled in behind foliage and latticed cane work.

Soon they were both drinking an iced John Collins. She had kicked off her shoes and tucked her legs up on the large sofa, looking him in the eye. "Tell me your thoughts then, pretty one?" She pushed the quiff of hair hanging over his left eye, off his face.

"I agree with Mickey," he sighed. "You could wear a potato sack and still look glamorous, Ma'am and I'm sure you tire of hearing it, but you do look especially lovely today."

This liaison was more profound than he had expected or even dreamed of at this stage, so it felt comfortable and natural once they were out of sight of the public.

"What about this hotel?" she said in her good-humoured and enlightening way.

"It looks Moroccan to me, Ma'am, probably because that's the only exotic place I've ever been to apart from this mad island so... African for sure. Definitely North African, I think?"

Without missing a beat, she said, "There are Moroccan, Tunisian, Algerian influences, agápi mou. Collectively called *Maghreb* if you remember? Don't you adore the whole Arabic leitmotif throughout the building?"

He shook his head in awe and gently brushed the back of his hand across her high cheekbone. She went on, "And although their rule was relatively short in the long history of these islands, the Arabs left a revelatory impact here."

As they both sipped their delicious, thirst-quenching cocktails, her eyes widened and she looked at him with intense desire over the slice of lemon and pretty little umbrella which now perched alongside that magnificent

Greek nose.

She spoke in a husky tone, "New techniques in irrigation were introduced and some of these are still visible on the landscape today. Perhaps we should go and look at them? Many of the place names in Malta date from this period too. This building has an Arab leitmotif throughout."

He flicked her hair back over her left ear and couldn't bring himself to say what he really wanted to say to her. But perhaps she knew what he wanted to say, and that was that he loved her passionately. She seemed to have felt like this when they first met and he was now on that same level with her.

"Yes... so exactly what is a leitmotif?" he said.

She squeezed his hand gently. "Leitmotif you say, agápi mou? I love the fact that the word can also turn up in different contexts, like in biochemistry, where it means a type of molecular sequence, but let's be honest, who really gives a fiddler's fig about that?"

He was spellbound. He cared about her funny little word and she knew he did, and so she carried on. "In works of art, though, a leitmotif is an element that appears throughout the work. It can be its theme or its main idea."

"I knew that!" he joked.

They both knew he didn't know and she waited for only seconds before he inhaled to speak, but she had started again before he could form those sounds in his head and exhale them as words. "But concepts like betrayal and forgiveness can be motifs too young man!" she said, her eyes boring into his. She was hypnotic. "A theme, agápi mou, is often used in design, such as a pattern or colour. A piece of fabric can have a floral leitmotif, a room may have a black and white one and a love song can have one too. This one," she leaned back and waved her hand in a circular motion, "is Arabic and I like it very much indeed."

His fiery eyes were becoming all too apparent to him, so he leaned back also and said with a casual honesty; "Leitmotif... it's quite an ugly word, isn't it, Ma'am?"

"Ugly? No, I would not say it was ugly, but it is

unbeautiful." How very beautiful that correction was, for him. "It's not a common word I know," she added, "but you know, I believe we should use it more." She sipped the long, iced cocktail so erotically to him, and then scrunched her nose up like a little girl. "I love the thought and I love the word. It is not mellifluous, and yet it is essential to me." She finished with a cheeky smile.

He had little idea what she had said and yet, he knew it was beautiful and she would explain more as she weaved it back into the conversation when she was ready. But the seed was sown.

The waiter put two more John Collins cocktails on the cane table without being asked, a gesture that, to Gideon, was the epitome of how things were done in foreign lands that he had only ever seen before at the cinema. Had the waiter just been waiting in the wings until she finished her speech?

He had started to speak when she suddenly sat up and slid closer to him, putting a finger vertically across his lips.

"I love you, Boy," she said in a creaky, broken voice as her eyes took on the sheen of tears. "We have to submit to the Moirai. I know you don't understand right now my love, but you will, I promise."

Both hands were wrapped delicately around his neck as she held him closer and he inhaled the aphrodisiac of her Patchouli scent. She pulled his head down onto her shoulder. "I love you so very, very much. I have a room here for us. Oh! The joy you give. What are we to do? *Siménis tósa polá ya ména*! That means you mean so much to me, Angel. And you do, you mean everything to me."

The 'I love you' had pierced his heart and her touch had a galvanising effect. *The Moirai* must be something from the mythical world she loved to talk about, and the idea merged delightfully into that alluring Greek language. Even her English vocabulary was sensuous to him now.

Just then, Mickey walked back in, strode to their alcove and picked up his cigarettes and lighter off the table. "Pardon me, Ma'am, forgot me fuckin' fags, didn't I? What a cunt, eh?"

He did an about-turn and walked away with the rolling gait of a seaman, now given the full Hollywood musical movie treatment! They laughed like two school children in a secret hideaway from an Enid Blyton story as he wiped tears from her cheeks.

Later, their lovemaking had a deep, romantic intensity in the refurbished but still seedy hotel room on that oppressive heat-soaked afternoon. Loving and meaningful, her eyes never left his as she began to moan with ecstasy, quietly and then screamed; "We are now..." she paused and panted before she caught her breath again "...one soul in two bodies' agápi mou. Ítan graftó na ímaste mazí," she whispered and then in English, "We were meant to be together," then back to Greek, "Ítan graftó na ímaste mazí!" She shook to her inner core as they exploded together and the stars cascaded upon them and the whole world paled into insignificance.

The melancholic tones from Mascagni's *Cavalleria rusticana*, the intermezzo, wept from the 1930s gramophone on the ancient dresser.

Gideon lay there with a glass of wine in his hand as she slept beside him. How did a youth like him find himself soaked in perspiration and entangled with this dream-like creature in this dusty, crazy city in the balmy Mediterranean?

He knew that what they were doing in that hotel was a court-martial offence in the Royal Navy, as Xanthe was a First Officer in the Women's Section of the Service. Also, in Catholic-controlled Malta in 1971, it was illegal to fornicate outside of wedlock – a mortal sin in the eyes of the Church.

Aromatic cooking smells, jasmine and hints of pine wafted through the windows and with the busy chaotic street sounds below, overwhelmed his senses. Only weeks ago, he had been seen as a boy; a West Country bumpkin. But this woman had shown him that a man couldn't grasp the elementary units of communication, in his case, his own language, what could he be trusted with? It had seemed so true when she had put it like that! He would carry the thought with him for the rest of his life. In this wonderful but complicated situation, he thought of himself as a man as he watched her naked stomach rising and gently falling with her breath. But what should he do next?

A drop of Nelson's blood down the Gut with Mickey, perhaps?

No, not as the afternoon turned into evening and the cicadas vied with the melancholic angst of the Soprano Santuzza, who was overcome by her jealousy of Lola, crackling from that old gramophone.

If the Ancient Gods were real, and for him in that moment, they had to be, then Xanthe was the *"to kalýtero apó ta kalýtera"* which was Greek for 'the best of the best.' It was pretty much the only Greek he knew.

So, no Nelson's blood for him today as a knock on the door woke the sleeping beauty and she quickly slipped her panties on, wrapped her silk kimono around her soft, chiselled body and went to the door.

She signed for the tray, which had a bottle of cold Chablis in an ice bucket on it. It came with a side order of frozen Chardonnay grapes, covered in ice, in an American Mason jar. She said with a calm air of authority, "This, young Sir!" twisting the bottle to show him the label whilst closing the door with her foot, "...is from the wine region in the northwest corner of Burgundy. It is a Chardonnay unlike other Chardonnays. It seldom uses oak-ageing, which means it has a very distinctive fragrance. And simply because of the reputation of Chablis, the unoaked style is becoming ever more popular all over the civilised world – which clearly includes here! This will alter your tastes forever."

"I've only ever had wine that you have given me, Ma'am. They sort of all taste the same to me, as nice as they are!" he said, screwing up his philistine nose.

"Then be prepared for angels to dance on your tongue for the first time, because this variation will change you after the first sip! Trust me!"

Truly, he did.

She poured an obscene amount into two Waterford crystal wine glasses and then dropped two of the frozen berries into each one. They chinked vessels and she wandered over to the bed. The glass met her lips and her eyes flashed as the pale golden liquid entered her body.

Resting her glass on the bedside cane cabinet, she untied her robe, exposing those minuscule white cotton laced panties. Muscled and olive, her flat stomach had him hypnotised in the dusky, sweet-perfumed room.

She slipped her Italian high-heels back on and sat on the edge of the bed and leaning backwards slightly, she gently inserted her finger into herself. Soon she was wriggling out of her flimsy underwear.

He tried to sip his wine, but gulped it instead. Christ, it tasted wonderful. He put the glass on the dresser, walked over to her and dropped to his knees between her legs, inhaling her magnificent aroma.

She whispered in a stream of Greek, which he didn't understand but which sounded incredibly erotic as she smeared juices from her finger over his top lip and gums and deeper into his mouth. He arose and entered her, and nobody now would ever take her place.

A drop of Nelson's blood? Not today, Mickey! Not today.

Chapter Two

Alone

In 1962, eight-year-old Gideon was enthralled by a child's adventure comic. Many characters sent him around the world, however his favourite was a dashing English World War Two pilot: a spiffing fellow full of righteousness. Another such character was an American motorcycle policeman who would crack a weekly crime with a random 'clue' for which the reader could search.

One particular week, the readers had to spot a villain amongst a typical crowd in a busy New York street. Since one rascal had a stripy shirt on, a beret and a sack over his shoulder with the word *Swag* on it, the boy thought that he must be detective material and his path in life was now chosen. He was amazed at his cleverness!

But it was the word that Americans used for milk that caught his attention in one frame of that story. A child had asked the ice-cream vendor for some 'moo juice.'

There were four farms in the quintessentially English village in Dorset where he lived, five if you counted the hamlet down the road. One of these farms was opposite the pub that was his home. His daily task was to get fresh, unpasteurised milk in a billy-can shaped like a milk churn, for the commercial kitchen. He loved milk more than anything else to drink and often thought that it was even better than food. Yes, he could live off that dairy delight forever.

One day as he handed over the small churn, he asked the kindly farmer's wife for some 'moo juice.' She smiled and said how amazing it was that such an Americanism could have reached a rural place twenty years behind the rest of the world.

Every morning after that, her greeting to him was always; "Good morning, young Moo Juice."

Even at that age, he disliked the name Gideon. There was nothing wrong with it, but he seemed to be the only person in the world to have this name, so instead of being proud of this individuality, he felt isolated by it.

When he grew up and became that lantern-jawed, dim-witted motorcycle cop's detective and superior, he would show him how to spot a clue, and when the rider was trembling in his boots, the smart detective would crack the case, signing off with; "Chief Inspector Moo Juice does it again!"

Being alone and ignored by one's parents had its advantages, and one of those was to be free to dream.

Gideon was brought up during the 1960s, although in his village backwater, the permissive society sadly passed them all by. His parents were both hard-drinking ex-naval personnel. Running an idyllic pub in the heart of the countryside kept their life full-on every single day. This left Gideon to wander by bicycle and foot all over the rolling hills, sometimes with a close school friend. But many times, happily alone.

Gideon was bright, and showed a keen interest in geography and history and excelled at football. What he did not have was guidance and more importantly, love. His older brother was his mother's favourite, and his cute, longed-for younger sister was his father's cherished one. Gideon did not mind this so much, but many times his father walked past him, steeped in alcohol, he would throw out a biting remark, which always included the words 'stupid,' 'idiot' or 'moron.'

The swipes that came in his direction were sometimes easily avoidable if he ducked away, but they were sadly intended to outsmart a child. On one occasion, the gin-fuelled father had hit him so hard when he was eating, that food was lodged in his windpipe. He collapsed on the dining table and after some immeasurable time, began to see distant white lights, but he felt no pain or fear. A warm feeling and a strange peace came over him.

Suddenly, he heard his mother screaming at his father as

the white lights disappeared and everything was upside-down as he found himself being held by the ankles and shaken vigorously. Then, dropped on the floor like a ragamuffin, he was sent to bed without finishing his meal. He found peace in his bed and a place to dream.

The pub was a business and his parents needed help, so there was a housekeeper and she was called Ruby. Ruby did the cooking, cleaning, housekeeping for the Bed and Breakfast side of the business and everything in between. She came and sat on Gideon's bed that terrible day and tried to explain to the frightened child that he needn't worry about anything.

The sooner he realised that his parents did indeed have their favourites, which made him special, then he could find comfort in other things, she said in her loving tone, as if she felt his pain. This made sense to Gideon. The problem here was that he found the comfort she spoke of, resting in her lap whilst she stroked his hair. It had a profound effect on him and he didn't want her to leave him. But she did eventually have to go and attend to her duties.

The next day and for most of the summer holidays, he couldn't wait to be with her. She lived some miles away and the county being rural, there were no buses or any form of public transport, so she had to be picked up every day by car and of course, taken home by Gideon's father. Much to the latter's annoyance, Gideon rode with them as often as he could. She would sit in the front and sometimes she would just reach back to touch his leg as a gesture of solidarity and the thing he needed most, a comforting reassurance. The driver was always too drunk to notice or, if he did, he didn't care.

At thirteen years of age, Gideon started to have physical feelings that he had not had before, specifically for this caring lady.

Ruby could immediately see what was occurring for him and acted appropriately. Her talks and guidance were soothing for him and he did and behaved as he was told, even though his yearning to be held by her all the time was burning deep inside his soul. It was a magical awakening for him to realise that there were wonderful people in the world who really cared about each other.

In that year, his ambivalent father brought the Royal Navy to Gideon's attention. He gave him a book called *The Boys' Book of the Navy*, written by a retired Commander and first published in 1953. It cost twelve shillings and sixpence – a huge amount to spend on a child.

His father had spent some years after the war sailing to the Far East, taking in the glory of the recent allied victory in the aptly named HMS Glory. This period in his life was never to leave him and he desperately wanted to get both his sons into that service, perhaps to relive his early life and the opportunities he had missed. The elder brother was not interested, but Gideon was hooked on the romance of travel and had, at the time, no idea of world politics or indeed the whole concept of 'working' for the Navy as a job. Life to him was going to mean *life* and not just a job; that much he knew after devouring this book.

In that birthday present, there was a photograph of a young seaman at the helm of the Cruiser HMS Kenya with the caption underneath saying, 'Every boy's dream, steering a modern cruiser!' How that made Gideon's heart skip. What a moment in his life: a light-bulb had flashed and there was no going back.

School had been wonderfully laid back, so that those who attended ran their own routine to suit their daily needs: which included mainly for the boys smoking cigarettes, chasing girls for a kiss and playing football once some of the basics had been covered!

Consequently, when Gideon went to join the Navy, he failed the entrance exam and it was the first time he had seen his father, or indeed any grown up, cry, except at the cinema. Having been expelled at fourteen for pushing a girl into the freezing cold outdoor swimming pool, he now went through intensive private tutoring to get the chance of a second crack at the exam.

He scraped in the next time, but it meant that he was to

be in an educational class once he arrived at the training camp in Shotley Gate in 1969.

The journey to the railway station to set off for his training passed in silence. His father left him at the drop off point without a word. He knew that he was leaving home for good, and that his father knew this too. His childhood died at that moment as he stood on the platform alone. The journey back to where he used to live was eleven miles long and with no means of getting there, his only option was to catch the train. His first lesson in life. There had been no excited packing, no goodbyes and no tears. It was how he had thought it would be, so it seemed natural to him. He spoke to nobody on the journey up to London and across the city to find his way up to Ipswich in Suffolk and report at the shore establishment of HMS Ganges. It was a Monday and it was raining.

He was fifteen years old, nervous and alone. There were no sandwiches, nothing to drink and the small bag he had with him only had a wash bag in it and some clean underwear. He had no money and, annoyingly, no handkerchief. Despite all this, Gideon felt good. Although he really did need to blow his nose!

Chapter Three

How could they be lovers?

Gideon had been a boy scout and camped all over his county, so he was able to mix with hundreds of other recruits.

There was no gentle easing-in period: the barking of orders was immediate. At lights out, a pair of recruits tried to run away from the compound and hitch a ride back home. This seemed bizarre to Gideon, who felt safe and warm and had no such thoughts. There was no comfort in going back to being disliked.

The four-week induction was at Shotley Gate, then a bleak, prosaic village on the windswept coast of Suffolk, in an Annex which was a satellite of the main establishment of HMS Ganges. A gruesome month, it was followed by a further nine months across the road. He was shouted at all day long in that sadistic period.

But no beatings. And amazing characters as friends.

Books had been written about the place with everyone finding a magic moment with a tear in their eye, and he had read them, but that all seemed like fantasy as they were subjected to total submission and degradation. An innocent remark could land the whole class in trouble.

Overpowering Parade Instructor: "On the other end of this stick sonny, is a miserable piece of shit!"

Trembling trainee: "Err, which end would that be, Sir?"

So, wearing their oilskins backwards and stiff, unbroken-in boots, unlaced, they doubled around the parade ground being told that the only thing lower than a whale turd was a Junior Seaman, 2nd class, who could not tell the right end of a stick. The whole class were included, because if the ship sank, they all went down!

If the county of Suffolk required an enema, this is where they would insert it, Gideon thought. They were drilled from sunrise to sundown with rigorous sporting activities in between. The subjects taught to them covered everything from the Augustinian monastic view of celibacy, through to sexually transmitted diseases and acts of bestiality between indescribable tribes.

This was all totally alien to a Dorset lad and the gruesome pace never once wavered for the ten months they were there. Importantly, they were taught that; 'Wisdom is Strength,' the Ganges motto which not only proved to be accurate but would stay with Gideon all his life.

They also became skilled in the art of oratory, to debate and question all this newfound knowledge.

Gideon as a raw recruit: "Excuse me, Chief, we only scrubbed this deck yesterday. Do you really believe that it needs doing again?"

Seasoned old Chief; "Sonny, thinking should be banned for a worm like you, because it does more harm than good. Your half-digested, bastardised Freudianism makes me think that you are on a perverse heading, and fifty press-ups might steer you back onto an even keel! Now then, are you filling in time or is there a point to your miserable, shitty fucking life? Get scrubbing. Move yourself! Move, move, move!"

How they went on to become complete masters of the sophisticated equipment of a fighting ship was a miracle. Some students thought that a Perspex dome under the hull and a pair of binoculars would detect a submarine quicker than the archaic Sonar type they trained on. However, they had a great feeling of superiority when they put on their much-envied uniforms.

Gideon was happy. Nobody beat him for no apparent reason and good behaviour, manners and a well-pressed kit were all rewarded, and so were his enthusiasm and dedication. To the Navy, he was an individual. Although he never had a West Country accent, he would naturally and gently roll his Rs, but he changed this overnight to by-pass the pigeon-hole naming system that would have given him a yokel-themed nickname.

He had had mandatory chores to do in the pub during the

year at home after he was expelled from school, including the constant filling of the coke-scuttle to stoke the Rayburn, their only source of heat. He also did a lot of bottling up, which involved lifting heavy wooden barrels, and all this had given him a well-toned body for a fifteen-year-old. This stood him in good stead amongst the other children at Ganges, as indeed, they were still very much just children.

The only journey away from the training establishment during those ten months was at Christmas. He teamed up with another boy to spend the leave period in London with his friend's parents, a kind gesture he would never forget. There were poignant moments in the capital as folk touched his collar for good luck, telling him what a gallant man he was.

The Navy had already taught him that just because he was born in a stable, it didn't make him a horse, and his friend's parents instantly ratified that statement. They appeared to be proud of them both, and meant it kindly when the first question they asked him was when was he going home to Dorset? He thought of his elder brother at home; he had always been distant and yet his cute little sister would be proud of him, he knew.

'Boys into men' was the Ganges mantra and it would seem that he had achieved that by the end of the training. The classmates performed like a well-oiled machine, as they clicked in and marched to the band and came to pass out. Their long-suffering instructor threw his stick on the ground and cried with joy. He had been a master of patience and leadership who truly moulded that class of '69, even when marching in the freezing, needlepoint rain.

Where were Gideon's parents on that passing out day? He had nurtured a faint hope that they might be there, but they didn't come. It was act of betrayal that would never leave him. The railway station on leaving home was a fulcrum moment but this was the dagger in his heart.

Was it right to be treated so harshly for so long? He knew that tight discipline was needed, and he had to take their age and the ideas of their generation into consideration. But why couldn't he have done the six-week basic training that sixteen-year-olds did down in Cornwall? Those recruits let their parents do the ironing and cooking for at least another year. Well, maybe that wasn't for him.

You're on your own now, he thought. And he greeted the idea with a smile, a warm heart and butterflies of anticipation.

Having been a senior at the Ganges for the last several months, he now became a junior again at HMS Vernon in Portsmouth, where he started his specialist branch training. Torpedo and Anti-submarine was the 'trade' he chose because the picture in the Naval Hand Manual, Book of Reference: 1938, issued to every recruit, painted a romantic view of the submarine hunters of the 1960s.

It was a time of significant changes in the Navy as computers were becoming dominant and the rum ration was being phased out. Well, the rum stopped dead in the water really. A two-and-a-half-ounce glass of rum and a few cans of ale when the sun came over the yardarm at midday did not help you to push the right buttons in the afternoon. Gideon had never believed that decades changed on the 'nines'; the fifties didn't really finish in 1959, or the sixties in 1969, but for the Royal Navy, 1969/1970 was a big turning point. The Labour Government of 1967 had started the demise of the Armed Forces and especially of his service, and it was now beginning to bite.

There was another turning point for Gideon too: in a strange way, he became a big brother to his older brother, Andrew. Gideon clapped eyes on him in the back of a naval bus, and it turned out he was arriving for his specialist training. Back home, his desperate parents had forced him to join the Navy to 'become a man' like Gideon. He had done the six-week course in Cornwall and now wanted to be a Sonar guy as well. They were affectionately called 'Taz-apes' and he wanted to ape Gideon, as it were, and achieve what he had already managed to.

They had never been close and Gideon had always thought Andrew was dim. As it turned out, he was just quiet and gentle and seemed to be seeking something just as Gideon was himself. Andrew had got a sixteen-year-old girl pregnant and had now been 'conscripted' into marrying her. "Yes!" he told Gideon, "Ma and Pa pulled some strings to get me next to you."

During his training, though, his puppy-dog look annoyed Gideon and he hated him hanging around trying to emulate everything he did all the time.

At the end of sixteen weeks, detail time came, or 'draft chits,' as it was known in the Navy. The ships in the fleet needing young talent were chalked up on a board and Gideon picked the one with the most romantic name, HMS Euryalus. Nobody could pronounce it, and no one knew what on earth it meant! An angry young Seaman in his class decided he did not want the ship he had picked originally; he now wanted the one Gideon had chosen, the Euryalus. Gideon was devastated but said "OK!"

Still, the instructor decided to toss a coin for the draft. The other boy got the first choice and chose heads. As he lost this one, Gideon forgot any feelings about this being OK. The Navy was treacherous! But it was tails second time and Gideon was back in the game. Now he got the final toss as the instructor said this was initially his ship, then he could proceed. He called tails again, and the ship was his.

Life is sweet sometimes, and his course was now mapped. Perhaps it was fate?

"Euryalus," their instructor told them, "was the son of Mecisteus. There is a statue of him by Jean-Baptiste Roman found in the Louvre Museum, Paris, France." The boys shrugged and looked bewildered. "It is called 'Nisus and Euryalus.' They were soldiers, but also lovers. The statue shows the moment when Nisus rushes over to Euryalus' dead body," the instructor added for Gideon's benefit, since it was well known that he liked history.

How could they have been lovers? Gideon thought. Surely they were both men? Maybe they had got that bit wrong.

Chapter Four

Jyoti the angel

So, with a big brown kitbag over his shoulder and a false rolling gait, Gideon arrived on the gangway of the Euryalus, a sleek grey messenger of death berthed in Devonport Dockyard, which was to become his base, on and off, for the next two decades. He was ecstatic.

The first deployment was to 'show the flag' for recruiting purposes. His illusions were shattered at this point as his former chums were spread throughout the world on their own ships, whereas his first port of call was Swansea in industrial South Wales.

They of the 'fighting fifteen' (the ship's pennant number was F15) hit the town and Gideon was accosted by an older, beautiful mature lady of Indian descent, who wore a tight tartan mini skirt and who he found extremely desirable. Gideon had never tried to engage with a girl, it just seemed to happen. He found that if they liked him, they would take the lead, and that's precisely what happened.

Slick and fast-talking, she neither knew nor cared for his name. She seemed to want just free alcohol all night, compliments on how attractive she was and real hard, mind-jerking physical contact at the end of it with no strings attached. He felt she got exactly what she wanted, and to his surprise, he felt strangely used afterwards.

Back onboard the next day, most of his shipmates were nursing hangovers and telling tales of the night before. Ziggy, a heavily tattooed northerner, was a natural-born comedian and had fallen off the pier looking for his cowboy boots. He had gone to kick an empty can and the right boot came off and spiralled into the darkness. He couldn't find it so threw the left one into the sea. At some point during all this, he had fallen off the pier. As he walked towards the gangway to return to the ship, there lying in the darkness was his right boot.

Big Knocker, a Londoner with a sarcastic wit so sharp he could cut himself, had a *ménage a trois* with a mother and daughter. And then there was Bomber, a quiet boy from Eastbourne who had fallen in love with a local girl. That lad would change beyond belief over the next few months.

Everyone Gideon spoke to agreed: it was the uniform that not only broke the ice, but did something to folk that was hard to explain.

The Chinese laundryman came sweeping through the mess deck in the morning, picking up their laundry. This was called *dhobi-ing* in the Navy, from the Hindu word for washing. He was screaming: "You filthy bastards, many stains, many stains!" The boys pinned him down, ripped his baggy pants off and simulated anal sex. He left in a hail of empty beer cans, screaming something in Mandarin about the afterlife and what their role in it would be. They were now cursed and they liked that very much.

When Gideon was drinking tea with Mickey from London that morning, his new mentor patted him on the back. "Giddy, good effort last night, but tonight, I want to get pissed and have a chat with you, so no women, eh?"

"But I've pulled duty today – I can't get ashore."

"Is that right, Mush?" Mickey sighed. "Wiggy, me ol' China! Stand in for Giddy tonight will you, we need a run ashore."

"Sure thing, Mickey," said a laconic old seadog, known as Wiggy-the-One.

On the town later, Gideon was watching the toilet entrance of a seedy pub on the waterfront while Mickey had sex with the landlady in a cubicle of the Gents. This in itself seemed to be no big deal to Mickey, but her husband was only thirty feet away behind the bar, with no idea of what was going on in his latrine.

Gideon himself had no idea until Mickey told him afterwards as they left the scene, laughing. Mickey was wondering what to call this dangerous sex? Did it have a name at all, and if not, could they make one up? Risky rutting? Hazardous humping? In the end, the hackneyed 'knee-trembler' was all Mickey could muster.

"Wow! Ace-to-base Mickey," said Gideon, amazed that people could be so casual.

"Yeah not bad, eh? And a looker to boot. Liked to talk dirty, that one. I have this theory about birds and stuff you know?"

"Everyone has a theory about birds, Mick."

"Nah, you sprog, birds as in tweet-fucking-tweet! Ever seen a bird shag?"

Where was all this going? How cool was this man? Gideon knew at that moment that he would never go back to Dorset. He was transfixed.

Mickey drew on his cigarette. "Well, I seen it on TV once. They kind of just fly at each other, touch for a second and whammo! That's it, the deed is done! Well, I got to thinking like, that a quickie can be good for both parties sometimes if the moment arises. Now, don't get me wrong and, most women like a cuddle and all that, but the type you and I will engage over the next two years is different! Not all mind, but some and you have to be ready when it comes."

Gideon thought of Ruby the housekeeper doing such a thing and his heart hurt.

"I'm here today to show you that it can work – like what I've just done. Now get the fucking beers in and we'll have a drop of Nelson's blood to chase that down with and none of that civvy shite either. Look lively, Gids, Uncle Mick is thirsty and remember, our motto is *Omnia Audax* and we must stand by that and defend it at all costs."

"I love it, Mickey. What does it mean?"

"I have absolutely no fuckin' idea."

Gideon nearly wet himself laughing.

The fifty-mile voyage across to Cardiff was gentle and busy with the hustle of life at sea. There were daily checks on the Sonar followed by constant maintenance on the upper deck, as salty air erodes everything in its path at an alarming pace.

The food on board was excellent, exotic and plentiful.

When the lads were not on watch, the evenings were lively parties playing the game of 'Uckers,' which was a bastardised form of Ludo. Sitting among these men and their tall tales made the young seaman laugh so loud, it made him physically ache. He would still be smiling at the colourful sea stories for many months. He loved the strong language and the laughter of seafarers at work.

He also loved the feel of the ship beneath him. She had become a living thing as the hum of her powerful engines drove her through the sea. Now considered a professional seaman, albeit on the lowest rung of the ladder, Gideon was part of a team. A family. He was told that if a machine or structure or even a vehicle had a name, it had a soul, which was something he could relate to. Euryalus, although a male in legend, was a 'she' now.

To Gideon, Cardiff was a tired place, still black and white compared to the vivid colour of London, Plymouth and other cities he had been to. However, everyone on board talked about how alive the place was, telling him of fascinating people who had two cultures, one of which was not only exotic, but also had a transcendental mystique.

In the Mortar Mk 10 bomb room, Mickey was banging on a cartridge with a two-pound lump hammer and scaring the hell out of the youngster.

"It's all true, son. The thing is Gids, the bleedin' Army was based in India for so long and many of these soldiers, or brown jobs as I like to call them, brought the natives back with them when we was told to sling our hooks." Gideon loved history and yet knew nothing much about his own island.

"Right horny some of them are too, I can tell you. Now then, don't be spooked by the boys' stories of mystique and all that because they are handsome for sure, but the problem comes when you fall for them. Easily done mind, but if you was to get spliced, they come with parents, two in number, grandparents, four in number and siblings... well, bleedin' dozens of them! *Omnia Audax,* my friend!"

"Mickey, what does that really mean?" But they all just

laughed heartedly.

Cardiff was a metropolitan city with a proud history and lovely people, including a substantial Indian population. Gideon and Bomber Wells were in a night club dancing when a couple of girls approached them. They were named Tanushree and Vimala and they were the third of their generation in Britain, and although their grandparents were from East Bengal, which was now Bangladesh, they said they were Welsh and both worked at Boots the Chemist.

Much alcohol and fumbling later, the friends said their goodbyes at the end of the gangway and the boys stumbled back on board for the night. Mickey was on duty at the gangway and said to Gideon that it was an offence to come back on board sober with no story to tell.

"Meeting them tomorrow Mickey, honest," he said.

"Good lad. What do you think?"

"They smell good, I've never smelled anything like it before," he said, slurring his speech.

"Right, get turned in you little shit, Uncle Mick will come ashore with you tomorrow."

The following day, Mickey had been ashore since midday and was down at the RNA Club waiting for Gideon, and Bomber was on duty, so Gideon went ashore on his own at around 1630 to meet Vimala at the back of Boots the Chemist. He rang the staff bell and a Bangladeshi vision from heaven called Jyoti came out to say that Vimala could not make it today and was not even in work. He tried to look tough as though he didn't care and was just thinking of catching up with Mickey when this lovely girl asked him to wait a minute and could he walk her to the bus stop? Whoa! For sure, Mickey could wait!

She never made her bus and they spent a couple of hours in a trendy pub talking about all sorts of stuff. He had never seen anyone so exotic and with so much thick black hair. As they sank into a haze of marijuana, all he could remember was stumbling up some stairs to her flat about 2200. He loved the smell there of Indian spices. How truly wonderful to him this was.

She kept 'shushing' him so as not to wake her flatmates as they slid into her bedroom, which looked like Gideon's idea of a brothel. Everything was red and gold. They sat on a carpet drinking cheap cider from plastic bottles and listening to the same type of music you got in every 1970s Indian restaurants, which Gideon had always thought of as tuneless, although it all seemed to be making more sense now.

Jyoti had a plan to be a boffin, she said. Gideon didn't know what this was and was too shy to ask. He said he liked that Indian word and she giggled. She started to explain that she wanted to be a chemist in a laboratory, testing, changing and re-testing different solutions for the pharmaceutical industry. Also, she said that the word 'boffin' came from the English armed services and was connected with technological research.

He liked this girl very much and admired her mind and ambitions. She was so cool and calm. Right then, he was in love with the whole mystical buzz and he felt that he wanted to go to India and melt into its culture. Jyoti got up and started to de-robe, and then she began to massage Gideon so gently in all the right places and for so long. When she turned him over to face her, his inexperienced hands were all over her and she gently pushed them away and told him that if he did that again she would handcuff him to the bedstead. Being a fool, he tried to hold her again and this soon had him shackled to the headboard.

She was so gentle and calm with him, like an angel. Then she straddled him and moved rhythmically up and down while all the time talking in Bengali. That strange language sent him on a journey to another place entirely.

They slept entangled like two serpents.

Chapter Five

The Rock and Africa

At around six in the morning, Jyoti woke and gently rubbed some sort of special oil over his face and neck, then kissed him passionately. They swapped addresses and before he left to go back on board, he put his head around the kitchen door to say hello to Jyoti's flatmates, and there were Tanushree and Vimala who both smiled and said, "Hi!" Gideon thought this was priceless!

The walk back to ship was long and cold. His main thought was that the address he had given Jyoti was HMS Euryalus, BFPO, ships. It was his home now. The thought warmed him up. Up and over the gangway, he went straight to the dining hall for a hot breakfast and sat down next to Mickey.

"How was your evening then, my young protégé?" said Mickey with a wink.

"Really blissful. She is such a nice girl. And I stayed erect for so long! I'm not sure what came over me?!"

"Well that'll be the hash you were smoking young fella, has that effect sometimes."

"How can you tell?"

"Cos, my rollicking, bollocking son of Neptune, you smell of patchouli oil to cover the original aroma. Dead giveaway Gids, get yourself in the shower toot-sweet, eh?"

"I think I'm in love, Mickey. No, really…"

"Well sorry to dampen your ardour, but the buzz is we've been detailed to a trouble spot somewhere in the world. You wouldn't want to miss that, would you? We have to get back to Plymouth to arm up. Don't look like that – remember our motto!"

"Stuff the motto!"

They both laughed. Mickey slapped him on his back playfully. His father never did anything like that. He felt more at home on the ship.

"Tell you what, Giddy, I'm bleedin' proud of you so don't get hung up on this girl. Think hard, but think from the head and not the heart, eh? Come on, let's go and see the Master at Arms."

The Master at Arms was the equivalent to the Chief of Police on board an English warship. He was usually either a really nice guy or a mean person on a mission to get as many haircut scalps on his office door as possible. There never seemed to a grey area between the two. Theirs was a pipe-smoking gentleman. Unusually, he had his jacket unbuttoned in his office most of the time. When things got serious, or he was about to reluctantly charge someone with a piffling 'offence' brought to him by an overeager officer, he would stand up and button up, looking annoyed at having to put his beloved pipe down for a minute.

"Morning' Master," snapped Mickey.

"Ah! There you are, young sirs. What can I do for you two, then?"

"Master, what does *Omnia Audax* mean?"

"Chuffed if I know, boys." He shrugged and sucked on that warm pipe which was to him like rosary beads to a priest. Rumour had it that although he loved his long-suffering wife, he preferred his pipe and wanted to be buried with it. He exhaled loudly and pondered for a moment. "Greek stuff, eh? If it is Greek? Maybe Latin? Chuffing complicated all that stuff and chuffed if anyone really knows. Like Greeks though, we like order and justice, fairness and good council, eh? And a good complicated motto!"

"Well, that really answered my question. Thank you for suggesting it Mick!" Gideon said as they walked away.

"You're welcome! Now get the fucking beers in and I'll tell you a tale that'll make your balls ache. I do know it is Latin, our motto, and here's another one you should know: Every man dies, but not every man lives."

Cardiff had been as good as Swansea for the lads and for Gideon too. He really had fallen for his Welsh girl. It did put a damper on everything he did after that moment.

Berthed back in Devonport to get everyone on a short leave, do essential maintenance and of course arm up, they found out that their destination was to be somewhere in the Mediterranean, although their superiors would not say where.

"Fuckin' Malta," was Mickey's guess.

"How do you know?" said Gideon.

"It's in the fuckin' papers, some Malt wants us out and replace us with their own socialist regime. Wankers."

"Maybe it's their time, Mickey, you know, run their own affairs and stuff."

"Look, Malta is a great run ashore, cos it's all left-handed out there and..."

"What do you mean, left-handed?"

"Catholics! They're called left-footers too cos all Irish navvies was Catholics, and they pushed their spades in with their left foot. It means everything is sort of underground, illegal if you like, and a bit dark. Which has its appeal, eh? We call them left-handers!"

"Everything with you is illegal, alcohol-related or immoral!" Gideon said with a smile.

"What's your fuckin' point?"

"Nothing, just an observation."

"Right, could be our last chance to lay some serious jiz down for Queen and country.

"What's jiz?

"Christ on a bike, sit yourself down Gids, me old China and Smudge, throw a couple of beers over here! Now then, *'Twas on the good ship Venus…*"

And all thoughts of Dorset, parents, pain and heartbreak vanished before Gideon's eyes as tears of hope and laughter engulfed him.

The day before they were due to sail, everyone was really charged. Married men were saying goodbye to wives, but not always their own wives; single ones were getting trashed down the strip. The mood was electric. Gideon was seventeen and the thought of it all was making him giddy.

About 1600 that day, Bomber and Gideon were just cleaning their paint brushes out and talking about the night ahead when a naval van pulled up at the end of the gangway. A new crew member jumped out to join the Euryalus and as he walked up the gangway Bomber says; "Scrub my old brown boots, look who it is!"

It was Andrew, Gideon's brother. Once again, their parents had pulled some strings with the Admiralty and had him drafted to the Euryalus to get him away from his young wife so Gideon could look after him. How Gideon clenched his fist and swore at the sky!

They set sail for Gibraltar and took three very stormy days to get there through the Bay of Biscay. On passage they did a period of 'plane guard' duty for an American Carrier which was carrying out the first deck landings of their new naval fighter, the F14. This was extremely exciting for Gideon as he was not at his beloved movie theatre now, but right behind this American leviathan, inhaling the very real smell of burnt aviation fuel.

What a fantastic sight that Rock was as they steamed through the Straight. Although under British administration, it still seemed very foreign to Gideon.

Mickey said that unless you got lucky with a Wren (the female force, then separate from the men's service), dating didn't happen on the Rock, so it was a place to get totally immersed in alcohol.

The first pub outside the dockyard gate was the Tartan Bar run by the first gay man Gideon had ever seen. It felt surreal to him as the boys mimicked this showman to the extreme. He thought of the 'Nisus and Euryalus' lecture back in Portsmouth and here it was before his very eyes. Men did love men! He could barely get his head wrapped around the notion.

Andrew's first child was born while they were there and 'wetting the baby's head' was a miserable and drunken affair for the brothers. They both ended up in a shore patrol wagon and Andrew was violently sick in the back as they hauled them back on board. Gideon was perplexed and angry with him. He knew this was wrong, but there it was.

The next day, although hung over, Mickey decided that he and Gideon would walk up to the top of the Rock to look at the African continent before they got smashed again in town. Rucksacks on, off and up they went and what a pleasant hike it was. When they reached the top, Mickey asked Giddy to get the beers out. He had not brought any beers, but unbeknown to him, Mickey had put a six-pack in his backpack. They were frothy and warm, but they were there!

Mickey told Gideon that he must take this vista all in, breathe it in too, because when you get old and infirm, all you have is your memories, and this would stay with him all his life.

"That's the fuckin' Africa continent, matey. Kinda hard to take in, eh?"

And truly it was one of the most powerful moments in Gideon's youth, looking at that continent from eight miles across the Straight from the top of the Rock of Gibraltar. Over-awed, his mind rushed to imagine, fix and realise that this was what he had been waiting for all his life.

His heart was pounding and he was about to say something immense when Mickey casually said, "Fuckin millions of lazy, good-for-nothing foreigners! That's what that place is." Gideon's face obviously gave away his thoughts and Mickey carried on; "Well, you're going to find out, me ol' China cos we'll be berthing there in Tangier next week. Fuckin' Moroccans, I hate 'em." And with that, they clanked their cans together and downed their beers.

Gideon could not find the courage to ask why Mickey was full of loathing for those folk. He thought of Jyoti and how Mickey had loved the thought of her.

They took the excellent cable car down into town and got drunk with the boys. It does not get much better for a young sailor from the back of beyond. After a week alongside the jetty, for some reason which mystified them, but as predicted by Mickey, they set sail for Tangier. Terrorist-orientated or political, they would never know.

But there they were alongside the African continent for rest and recreation.

Mickey launched into a long lecture about women not being available here unless you paid for them, which surprised Gideon at first, but Mickey said it was well worth it. As always, he seemed to be in the know.

"Get your lagging on, Wonder Boy, you are in for a treat. It's going to be like all your birthdays have come at once, you'll never forget it."

Gideon was already overwhelmed to have left Europe for Africa. What could be waiting to thrill his senses next?

Chapter Six

Mickey the Oracle

That short trip across from Europe to noisy, bustling Tangier was uneventful but full of excited anticipation. Gideon noted his thoughts as they berthed alongside an old, dilapidated pier with Moroccans in attendance in their long robes and battered old western blazers and hacking jackets which made this look like a 1920s movie set. Nothing could have prepared Gideon for the smells, the colours, the people, and the profound change in culture.

His immediate thoughts upon berthing were of sadness. Silly, he knew, but that is precisely how he felt. How could people be so poor?

The Moroccans turned out to be quite lovely and proud of their traditions. They were tribal and protective in the extreme and gave the impression that they had chosen to be where they were at that particular time on the world stage.

As some Moroccan naval personnel were being shown around the Euryalus, they seemed to be impressed with modern radar and other sophisticated equipment, but the European lifestyle caused them bewilderment, especially the alcohol in the bars and messes.

"They're technically Arabs, Gids," Mickey said. "Proper Darkies live further south…"

Gideon wondered what sort of education he was getting here. He thought of Jyoti again.

The first time ashore, they entered the walled part of the city called the Medina and went down narrow alleys that tourists were discouraged from visiting. They went all the way through to the other side where they were stopped by a mean-looking Arab with a scar by his left ear – straight out of Hollywood. Mickey informed this buccaneer that he had a cherry boy to pop and the Arab's eyes lit up. "Special price for you, my friend, I have an *Ouled Naïl*," he says to Gideon.

31

"What's an *Ouled Naïl* Mickey?" he mouthed over his shoulder as he climbed the rickety stairs on the side of the building.

"On you go, sonny, follow the cut-throat and remember, I'm right here in this café, you lucky bastard!" he guffawed as he grabbed his private parts in a Neanderthal gesture.

There was, bizarrely, a small white washed room on the roof top. Gideon entered the space, which immediately smelled lovely, and two women sat there, the elder in a hijab and the younger wearing a niqab. There were white-painted walls with clay pots and heavy drapes, and incense sticks burning in their dozens made for a heady ambience. Surely he was now on the set of *Casablanca* and Humphrey Bogart was going to walk in soon?

The old woman was speaking in Arabic and from her gestures, he understood that he had to get undressed. The young tribal lady had stripped down to her highly decorated niqab and he had never seen a more erotic thing before. She had tattoos of what looked like fern leaves all over her body. These were so very delicate and beautiful that he wished he could decorate himself with them too.

The older woman was sitting next to the bed. Whatever did she want? The younger one beckoned him to lie down and Gideon was thinking that for his two main sexual experiences, the woman had taken charge and that's what was happening here.

She then proceeded to straddle him almost in slow motion. He looked up at her and with only the niqab on, her eyes were so predominant and magical and he stared into those sparkling green and black pools and whispered, "Jyoti." Sad, romantic young fool, he thought.

It seemed that anything was available except kissing. After lengthy, slow-motion, dream-like sex, there was a massage which involved the girl chewing on a mango or a peach and bits would be spat out over his body and massaged in with the oil. He had no idea what for, but he sure as hell smelled good!

As he fell back onto a big decorative cushion, the elder

mopped his sweat-covered brow. He really would have told her to go away, but she seemed to be part of the deal.

"You are beautiful," he said to the girl. He was weak but satisfied and calm with the total release. From films he knew that this was the part where he slept for an hour, only to be woken by lovely nymphs and taken back on board by eight of them, all strewing rose petals in front of him as they carried him up the gangway for all to see.

Actually, the elder clapped her hands. *"Finny, finny"* she shouted, shooing him away down the rickety stairs. He looked back to catch a glimpse of the beautiful one, but she has disappeared behind some drapes. Gideon flipped his cap back on at a rakish angle and walked back into the bar below.

"What kind of bar is this then, Mickey?"

"Fuckin' Moroccan bar, you mollusc. How was it then? Did you get your money's worth?"

"Yes, because she was so very spectacularly pretty and she thought I was cute, and, you won't believe this, I got it for free, Mickey. Honest! Not a dirham changed hands! Cool, eh?"

"You total prick, I paid Scar-face before you went up, I get a special price with a couple of free beers chucked in cos it's a business thing innit? So how was it?"

"Surreal."

"What the fuck does that mean?"

"Umm, kind of misty, somewhere between real and not real."

"Too many books you been reading Gids, stick with Uncle Mick."

"Well, I can now understand what toe-curling means because my toes really did start to curl," Gideon said, shaking his head.

"It's a spasm thing, does happen if you get the signal from the brain. Orgasms come from the brain, not your dick." Gideon gazed on this Oracle, smiling in anticipation of the wisdom coming his way. "Well, your dick is your dick for sure and a bloody useful tool it is too, my young friend, but real balls-aching moments that make you black out for a second or two are from visual and sensual feelings that come through the eyes, nose and throat. Your brain interprets them as special or whatever, and that triggers an orgasm. You can always shoot some jiz, it's what wanking is for, but orgasms, well, different thing altogether, eh? You have to pay for that."

"So, what about your wife and stuff then Mickey? Don't mean to pry."

"Comes with the life, matey. We ain't got nothing in common. She knows the stuff I do and we're all right in the big picture of life, but deep, meaningful sex is confined to foreign trips. Ask yourself this, when did you ever have a fuck like that back in the UK?"

"Well, back in Cardiff, actually."

"Don't be a clever twat, you sprog. The smells and bells of this place and the fact that you never get to see their faces, the smokes – fuckin' totally cosmic!"

He had a twisted point. They drank ice-cold beer and Gideon raised a bottle to his father, the publican who would not have believed how these wonderful folk served beer.

Mickey went off to the toilet and Gideon eased back into his big cane chair and thought that maybe he had already surpassed his father's experience of life in the Navy. He tried to think of things they had done together during his childhood. His mind was blank.

Tangier was a fabulous place and he ached with the satisfaction of sex, hash and alcohol that hot afternoon. He thought of Mickey and was about to think of something beautiful to say to him, or perhaps to ask why he was so opinionated about everything.

Just then, Mickey returned. "The dark continent, matey! Fucking dark as it gets, but not as dark as the shithouse I've just been too!" He winked, and Gideon spat his beer out laughing.

He wondered about the English perception of their Christian God and what that God thought about Mickey? He looked at the old salt who had a cigarette in the corner of his mouth and was chattering on about just about everything in this world appertaining to the opposite sex. Gideon would have followed him anywhere.

Chapter Seven

The Catholics and the Gut

Suddenly, HMS Euryalus sailed for Malta the next morning.

That year, 1971, the old monetary system of pounds, shillings and pence had ceased to exist back in the UK, to be replaced by decimalisation. This had confused Mickey's maths converting dirham (the currency in many of the Arab states) back to Sterling. He was also angry at the loss of that wonderful florin coin. The florin was also called a 'two-bob bit' which was funny to him as it was his rhyming slang for going to the toilet.

With this in mind, Mickey and Gideon discuss world problems and their role in it all and how coinage could be debased.

"A horse, a horse, a kingdom for my horse," Mickey quoted. "True innit, Gids, crossing the desert ain't no chuffing good without a beer, eh?"

"Or a glass of water Mick or indeed a chuffing horse?" They fell about laughing.

The public address system crackled: "Tricky situation here chaps," the Captain boomed.

"Not sure what to expect or what our role will be, but we are first in, so the eyes of the world will be on us, you can count on that. *Omnia Audax* and all that, God willing, what!"

The Captain rambled on about the word dignity and how history would record their behaviour in this delicate situation. The ship was in constant touch with London as the involvement of the British on the island came to a political close.

Malta was an important place for the UK and it had been awarded the George Cross for bravery during the Second World War for fighting on when Germany and Italy tried to crush the British presence there through bombing.

There was a big Army contingent on those islands, as well as an RAF Air Station, and not only a naval base, but a naval dockyard too. Large numbers of British servicemen and women were based there: 3,500 service personnel with over 7,000 dependants. And all were to be ousted overnight, it seemed. HMS Bulwark, a commando carrier, was on her way, but would not arrive for at least a few months due to commitments elsewhere.

"What a clusterfuck," Mickey said as they were about to start the evacuation.

The Euryalus crew were excited as 7.26 self-loading rifles were brought out, and they shot over the stern at floating targets to practise their weaponry skills.

A helicopter was scrambled in what seemed to be a dramatic sabre-rattling exercise. The British knew what kind and gentle folk the Maltese were. If we had to go into 'combat' they thought, then hell, this was the way to do it, gently and with certain sadness.

The Euryalus stayed just over the horizon overnight and sailed into Grand Harbour at exactly 0800. The view of the entrance with its old forts was breath-taking and the sea-tinged air in their noses was replaced by that unique Maltese combination of spices, enhanced by the Biblical buildings, and the sounds of busy, dedicated folk with a proud heritage: Mediterranean, but unlike any other country beside that sea.

Gideon was on the bridge deck-head as a member of the piping party with Bomber, so he had the best view of the place as they arrived. He had a deep feeling of anticipation and excitement as the ship berthed alongside HMS St Angelo. Everyone was 'fallen in' and lined up on the ship in perfect naval tradition. Mickey was walking aft down from the forecastle and looked up at the two boys. He grabbed his penis through his bell-bottoms, winked and shouted up, "Gonna give those Malts some teasing tonight, eh!"

Bomber said to Gideon; "Wanna swap Sea Dads,

matey?" Bomber's mentor was a sensible, warm-hearted Leading Seaman of Polish origin nicknamed 'Jazz.'

"Can't do that, Bombs, ever."

"Why not?"

"Because he *is* my Dad now, I don't think blood is thicker than water any more. He might be right about tonight, too. He says the Catholics here have done us a favour by making sex a sin."

Malta was a group of seven islands in the heart of the Mediterranean, and boasted a rich tapestry of archaeological and cultural treasures. It had some of the oldest prehistoric structures in the world – so all sorts of impressions hit the seamen as they arrived and settled in. But if there was one word to sum up the place, it was Catholicism.

The island was totally Catholic, without any room for manoeuvre. The juxtaposition of the almost entirely Maltese population with the massive influx of British service personnel and their modern, worldly ways was striking. For the new arrivals, the biggest hurdle was that the religion they had to work with over the next few months sometimes clashed with theirs through no fault of either denomination. Difficulties arose.

It started during the first run ashore. About eight mess mates, all young, fit sailors, had been drinking in the canteen on the base and then they stepped ashore for an all-night session. Gideon joined them.

They were in a bar in the town of Sliema much later and the comedian among them, Ziggy, was becoming amorous towards a charming, chaperoned girl. Mickey, forever the leader, had a quiet word with Ziggy who was usually very well-mannered and cool. However, he had the hots for this unattainable lady and would not let it go.

Mickey said, "You got to back off Matey, she's a proper left-hander, make no mistake, and there's plenty more of what we want where we're going later. Life, me ol' China, is like a pubic hair on a toilet seat, you often get pissed off! Live with it. Move on."

Ziggy screamed in drunken jest, "Jesus-H-fucking-Christ-on-a-bike, Mick, you're going to tell me she doesn't take it up the arse next!"

They all howled with laughter, Neanderthals and proud. Gideon laughed too but the embarrassment on the girl's face shamed him.

The mention of an anal sex act could land you jail in Malta and the key would be thrown away forever, but it was the reference to Jesus on a bicycle that ended their time in that establishment. In the ensuing mêlée, with the Shore Patrol in attendance by now, Mickey laid two guys out, Ziggy accidentally trashed the glasses on the bar as he tumbled over and Knocker broke a chair. Gideon tried to protect the girl from the fight and her Maltese uncle punched him in the face, thinking he was about to hit her. Gideon defended himself by retaliating. They were all taken off by the Patrol Unit to cool off in jail for the night.

No charges were brought against them except payment for the damage and thankfully, the authorities were sympathetic. Gideon had to apologise to the Naval Shore Patrol and his fine was in the form of many cans of beer sent to that Patrol the next morning. Alcohol was not bribery, it was a currency.

After the Second World War, Malta had achieved self-rule and sought full integration with the UK. Some of the natives favoured independence but asked for the same dominion status that Canada, Australia and New Zealand enjoyed. In 1955, the Maltese cabinet came to England, led by socialist Prime Minister Dom Mintoff, and asked to be a satellite of Britain with representation in parliament, and to share social services so they could escalate their standard of living to equal that of the British.

The same Mr Mintoff was re-elected in 1971 and immediately set out to renegotiate post-Independence military and financial agreements with the UK. They couldn't agree on major issues, and this had culminated in full British withdrawal and full Maltese independence.

To get into Valletta from St Angelo, Gideon and his

mates took a beautiful boat ride across Grand Harbour in a small gondola-style craft called a *dghajsa*. This water-taxi landed at Lascaris Wharf, where the old Customs House used to be. They took the rickety ride up the Barrakka Lift, which had opened in 1905 and clearly hadn't been maintained since! It stopped at the Upper Barrakka Gardens, which offered a shorter and quicker route to Valletta's centre.

You might think they would have been keen to learn about the island's rich history after hundreds of years of being conquered by Sicilians, Phoenicians, Romans and more recently, the British. But no, like most sailors, they headed to Valletta's Strait Street. This narrow conduit was easily the most famous street in Malta for service people from any country. Known as *Strada Stretta* in Maltese, the road had been the pinnacle of nightlife amongst British military personnel since the 19th century.

Strait Street, known as "the Gut" to British sailors, represented a fascinating period in Malta's history in which people of different nationalities and classes intermingled in a social context. This was a new kind of multiculturalism, one that was different from previous centuries of simply being dominated by power after power. It was more integrated, more inclusive. Strait Street became a hub in which the British and Maltese could co-exist in harmony.

Before Gideon and the crew went ashore, a Liaison Officer had attempted to explain Maltese thinking to them.

"The Maltese believe in the scriptures, totally. The Bible says in Leviticus 2013, 'If a man also lies with mankind, as he lieth with a woman, both of them have committed an abomination: they shall surely be put to death; their blood shall be upon them!' And the book of Deuteronomy 22:13 — 21 say: 'A marriage shall be considered valid only if the wife is a virgin. If the wife is not a virgin, she shall be executed.' Verse 21 states verbatim: 'Then they shall bring out the damsel to the door of her father's house, and the men of her city shall stone her with stones that she die: because she hath wrought folly in Israel, to play the whore in her father's house: so shalt thou put evil away from among you.'"

Stoned to death for not being a virgin on your wedding day? Gideon figured that all the girls down that conduit were never going to heaven now! Although he soon discovered that most of the girls plying their exotic trade there were not Maltese. The Gut was a different 'state' than the rest of the island.

On most of the island, nice, well-to-do Maltese debutantes were known as *rare birds* and *damsels* and they only ventured out to enjoy entertainment in the better establishments, usually chaperoned by both parents. Strong rumour had it (backed up by the Liaison Officer) that if a man secured permission to dance with one such *damsel* three times in succession, this would be virtually a proposal of marriage! Some servicemen actually hunted out such places to find a woman who would be kind and gentle, as this was how they imagined the perfect wife. The romantic in Gideon had no problem with this and indeed, a young stoker from the Euryalus did precisely that and as far as he knew, lived happily ever after in Bristol!

Strait Street's reputation stemmed from its sheer contrast to the Catholic Malta that encased it. The Gut had a nightly routine involving drunkenness, rowdiness, prostitution, and cross-dressing. Everyone loved it.

Chapter Eight

Byordermod

Now temporarily drafted into HMS St Angelo, Gideon spent a week travelling the island, handing out boxes so that the families of servicemen and women could pack up. He was also involved in commandeering military equipment that would be transferred to the Commando carrier that was due in.

At the end of the week, he and two other Able Seamen formed a small working party with Mickey in charge, at the Communication Centre in the Lascaris War Rooms in Valletta. In 1967, this had become NATO's strategic centre for processing the Soviet interception of submarines in the Mediterranean and they were there to remove the sensitive communication equipment, or at least to close down outdated systems, as guided by the Royal Navy staff there.

The party was headed up by an aloof young Sub-Lieutenant called Mr Hinkley, who had been drafted from England to HMS St Angelo temporarily. He was attached to the Euryalus for several months as an extra hand while the initial quirks of the withdrawal were taking place. As the days unfolded, there were new and demanding challenges.

The diminutive Mr Hinkley was uppity and supercilious, and undeniably using his superior education in a bullying way. There was a rumour on board that he was some sort of minor aristocrat. He clearly assumed that talking to the Maltese, who he saw as an inferior race, was beneath him. They were all looking at an old teleprinter with a chit taped to it in the Signal Office whilst Mr Hinkley was being rude to a Maltese official, talking down to him without thinking who he was talking to. Gideon and the team wondered why it was necessary to be so didactic at that initial stage, or any stage for that matter. The Maltese gentleman was having none of this and his expression and shoulder shrugging conveyed this beautifully.

"I have to act," Mr Hinkley said, "before this treacherous race start using the teleprinter to communicate with the Russians." It was a joke that no one found funny.

It turned out later that the Maltese gentleman was tasked with managing the building after the British finally pulled out, but Mr Hinkley had no idea of this, and no authority to speak to anyone in his arrogant and outdated manner. Mickey, the two Able Seamen and Gideon were appalled and embarrassed.

Mr Hinkley barked "That one!" and pointed out the ancient printer to Mickey, who immediately told the officer, in front of the team, that it was out of date and unserviceable.

"That ain't going nowhere, Sir!" he concluded.

"Why would one assume that, Leading Seaman King?" Mr Hinkley asked.

"With respect, Sir, fucking says so on this chit taped to it! It says that the fucking thing is fucking well fucked, Sir, and to leave it here! Orders from some knob called Byordermod, Sir!"

Apart from the sniggers, the silence was deafening. Then the beleaguered Maltese official agreed that it could be left behind as it would be of no use to NATO or indeed, those pesky Russians. How they all beamed.

"Alright, alright!" said Mr Hinkley, knowing now that the local man was teasing him.

"And Sir," says Gideon, "it was ours, but being unserviceable and out of date, it's useless to us, but left here, it becomes their history. Win-win situation and we all go home happy."

Mr Hinkley pondered for a moment as though he was about to swim against the tide again because of the honest, but insolent input from Gideon.

But at that moment a mellifluous female voice spoke from immediately behind Gideon. "The young Seaman is correct Nigel, there are plans to make this building into a museum and what an ideal opportunity to keep this original encrypting machine in situ. It would be purposeless to take it back to the UK."

Mickey and Gideon turned. There was a female First Officer, a Wren of the British Navy, the equivalent of the male Lieutenant-Commander, with two and a half rings on the epaulettes of her tailor-made white uniform.

Something else about her made Gideon's heart skip a beat. There was an eerie silence for a few seconds and in the cave-like environment, there was a slight echo of her voice, as if they were on stage in some old opera house, he thought. He had never seen such a beautiful, Arabic-looking woman. He could smell her warm, soft, vaguely familiar scent because she was extraordinarily close to him.

Gideon turned back to Mr Hinkley. "Ma'am is right, Sir. When your children come back here on holiday, you'll be able to say that that piece of history is there because you ordered it. It will confirm across the world that England isn't all bad, because of people like you, Sir! Do you remember Geronimo at the battle of Little Big Horn, Sir? Didn't he say that it was a good day to die before going into the fight? I don't think it's a good day to die, but maybe it's a good day not be hasty, Sir?"

Mr Hinkley looked angry, but grudgingly capitulated and barked another order at Mickey. Off they went through the tunnels, leaving the chipped, clapped-out machine that had clattered away there since the 1950s, in its dusty old corner.

Gideon turned back towards the vision in white and mouthed, 'Thank you.' She gently closed her eyes and lowered her head as if to say, 'You are welcome.'

Wasn't life perplexingly beautiful sometimes? Gideon had no idea what had happened, but something had awakened inside and now engulfed him. If he had never saw her again he knew that he would spend the rest of the day just thinking about her because of the look he had seen in those eyes.

Even so, there was work to be done and the rest of the morning was spent in the tunnels doing various tasks. All exciting and all different. The team were just heading back on board, Gideon and Mickey the last to leave with their Land Rover, when the First officer slid back into the foyer to thank them.

"So you like American Indians do you, agóri?" she said to Gideon. He was paralysed. He hated himself for it, but there was a certain flush within him that he had never had before. She spoke with a gentle kindness, "I have read that 'It's a good day to die' was a common saying, but unlike in the movies, it was not Geronimo, Crazy Horse or even Low Dog who said it. The Sioux did have a war-cry to that effect, though, '*Hoka-Hey!*' which they used to show that they were ready for whatever came. Your protection of the vulnerable was admirable when you quoted it. Indeed, it's never a good day to be stupid, is it?" She said this with the warmest smile he had ever seen.

Mickey looked perplexed.

"Is something wrong, Captain?" she said, teasing him with that rank.

"Yes Ma'am, is that fucking Hinkley ponce really called Nigel?"

She blushed at his vulgar honesty, but she was still smiling.

They bowed and walked backwards in a mock-subservient way, holding their caps as if to say, 'We don't have the right to even be looking at you!' The First Officer put her hand over her mouth to stop herself from laughing.

On the ride back around the harbour, Mickey said, "What's with all that Pow Wow shit, Giddy? And why Geronimo?"

"Well I read about it – I'm interested in all that American history. Didn't I look stupid, though, naming Geronimo for Christ's sake? It must have been that parachute joke you told me about, you know, the one where the sailor jumps out of the aircraft and screams *Geronimo*!"

"Yeah! Funny as fuck that one eh? Scrub me ol' brown boots, though, she's a looker, and a Bubble too I think? I like them Bubbles."

45

Gideon simply had to ask who Byordermod was and Mickey said, "Some twat in the Ministry?" before letting on that of course it meant By Order of MOD.

Byordermod became a euphemism for anything on the mess deck ordered from the MOD, or any task they were given that was just silly and inexplicable.

And Mickey thought she was a Bubble? Gideon decided he didn't need to know what that meant right now, in case it was something unpleasant.

Chapter Nine

The Sisters of Fate

Gideon was having a cup of lime juice the next day, which was searingly hot – too hot to work past midday, which was for certain.

The Sub-Officer of the Day was Mr Hinkley. At around 1000 hours in the morning, he had the Quartermaster call Gideon to the gangway over the tannoy system. Gideon thought this would be a nice break for a bit as they were about to rig the awnings to stop the sun burning the metal decks of the ship. When he arrived on the flight deck, the Quartermaster said there was a visitor who wanted to see him and there, standing by the Mortar Mark 10 and talking to the Officer of the Day, was the female First Officer from yesterday.

Gideon stood some fifteen yards away and waited. The woman was devastatingly attractive and her hair was as dense and as black as he has ever seen. Thickly plaited, it was pulled up and back and secured with a Greek-keyed silver sword and shield clip. Her uniform was clearly handmade and showed off her slender figure and unblemished olive skin. Eyeliner darkened her eyelids and embellished those arched eyebrows, protecting insanely long eyelashes and dark eyes, to make sure one had nowhere else to look. She looked like Cleopatra to Gideon.

Mickey climbed up the ladder from the mortar well and onto the flight deck, saluted the First Officer and said, "Morning,' Ma'am!" As he passed Gideon, he whispered, "Gawd all fucking mighty... now that's arse to wake up next to, eh, Gids? A proper Bubble an all, she gives me a hard-on!"

Gideon was smiling when she had finished talking to the Officer of the Day and he had bowed slightly and walked away. She gestured to him with her finger to approach her. She was cultivated and decorous and when he was in front of her, he noticed for the first time that those eyes were impossibly black with flecks of blue.

"Good morning, young Sir!" she said in a husky tone. "I wanted to convey the warmest thanks of the Maltese official who you helped so kindly yesterday. These can be difficult times and your wonderful intervention was lovely to watch."

"I just don't like injustice, Ma'am and Mr Hinkley was sort of arrogant and silly. I think Leading Seaman King handled him better than me and it might have come across as disrespectful, but ignorance and stupidity have to be handled in different ways and Mickey's was the right way, I think?"

She smiled. "Quite so." How very charming, and so very English, he thought.

"And I have learnt that it is an overwhelming ignorance to suppose that other people around the world think the same as the English do. I mean, even the Scots don't think like us, so why would the Maltese?" He wanted to be bolder, even though he felt slightly weak at the knees. That's just a cartoon saying, he thought, but he really was shaking a little. "What brings you here this morning, Ma'am?"

"I'm with four of my Chime and shall be leaving around 1300 hours and I wondered if you were around to say goodbye or…" She moved slightly closer, briefly looked around and whispered, "Or needed a ride?"

Goodbye? Say goodbye? Needed a lift? Say goodbye? Indeed, alarm bells should have rung.

"Yes, Ma'am, it was lovely to meet you again. Truly," was all he could burble.

"Lovely to meet you?" and "Truly?" Shit! That was disrespectful to an officer, even though she was clearly OK with the rapport.

Sensing his discomfort and dilemma, she said: "Why don't you walk to the small island in the square just down the road and I will pick you up on my way through as I am going back to Ta'Xbiex after Luqa? You can tell me of your passion for the Native Americans and I do want to hear

48

about that beautiful rapscallion Leading Seaman King. Let us say I leave here around 1300 so around 1430 at the square?" She raised her eyebrows, leaned slightly towards him again and whispered, "Please be there. Tell nobody. I risk everything for this. I can see you are a man of probity. I believe in the Sisters of Fate."

Now he was in trouble. And whatever did 'probity' mean? His addled brain came out with; "Aye Aye, Ma'am!" and he did a one-eighty and slid down the mortar-well ladder all professional, cocky and seaman-like.

Work detail was piped to finish at 1145 and he was in that shower at 1146 and then into mufti and he walked up to the quarter deck at around 1300, trying to look calm and relaxed as if he didn't care about anything, save the fantastic view across the harbour.

At 1305, the First Officer arrived back on the flight deck with four lower-deck Wrens and walked across to see if he would be on that corner of the square? She reiterated that she had to drive to the RAF Station Luqa to drop the other four off first and as it was only three miles down the road, it would only take an hour or so.

Nobody could hear what they were saying and he said yes of course and then casually stated that he didn't really need a lift as the *dghajsa* were hovering at their stern and he could just hail one. His attempt at acting mature had failed. She knew it and so did he, but he then said quickly, "Of course, a lift would preferable, Ma'am."

She smiled so warmly that it took his breath away, just like in the soppy movies he watched all the time. He pulled his shoulders back and hoped his now grown-up expression conveyed a cool attitude. Mother of God, he was rubbish at flirting with someone so far out of his league.

Without another word or look between them, the five women saluted the Officer of the Day, descended the gangway and boarded the iconic dark-blue Royal Navy Land Rover. Off they went, driven by the First Officer herself through the narrow streets.

The Officer of the Day, a lieutenant, asked Gideon what

that chat was all about? He said that Mr Hinkley had lodged his displeasure at Gideon being a smart-arse to him the day before, and now he resented a superior, albeit a woman, talking to an oik.

Gideon told him the truth. "I just backed her up yesterday, Sir, you know, that lady officer… it was an awkward situation and I tried to protect the Malt. She just said she was grateful for that."

He shrugged. He knew his place, but he had pissed off the jealous aristocrat and that made Gideon feel good. Of course, the Lieutenant was smart enough to see the situation as it was. They were the cutting edge of the dying Empire and Mr Hinkley had not yet learned the ways of fairness.

Back down to the mess deck Gideon went, and told Mickey his tale of woe.

"For fuck's sake, Gids! Right, get yourself properly ship-shaped and I'll walk you off the gangway, but this has to be a one-off, and if you're caught, then only God bleedin' helps you! Craven the Raven, eh?" he said with an evil grin.

"What?"

"Her name is Craven and she has raven hair, stands to reason don't it?"

At 1420 Mickey and Gideon, along with a few other ratings, walked down the gangway onto the jetty. All turned left for a *dghajsa*, except Gideon and Mick who turned right and walked into Birgu. They waited at the end of St Edward Street. It was hot and dusty and everything looked sepia-tinted and charming as if it were refusing to let the world catch up with it, though it surely would soon.

They stood there for some time, and then the Royal Navy Land Rover clattered to a dusty stop and a creature of unparalleled beauty looked at Gideon and said, "Jump aboard, sailor boy!"

Mickey gawped. "Jesus-H-Christ-on-a-bike, Gids!" He brushed him down like a mother leaving a child at the school gate and proudly turned him around to face her. "You look after him Ma'am as the little shit is all I have to beat and vent me frustration out on!"

She smiled and Gideon knew that all was well with the world.

Gideon turned to express his gratitude and Mick whispered: "Don't fuck it all up, matey. Meet me in the bar next to the Green Doors later, eh? And if you get lucky, what time do you have to be back on board?"

"O-seven-thirty."

"*Zero* seven thirty. 'O' is what your mother sighs when I fuck her. Now off you go!"

Gideon couldn't stop laughing at this mad character who had selected him for his initiation to all things nautical.

As they pulled away, Mickey shouted; "Green Doors!" The Green Doors he knew was a house for women of tarnished virtue in Strait Street. Forever classy and thoughtful was this mentor. With that, Mickey skipped back towards St Angelo and Gideon slid into the seat next to the First Officer.

"What are the green doors, agóri?" she asked as they drove away.

"It is a bar with rooms that entertains sailors, Ma'am," he said with embarrassment. "It, um, has green doors..."

"Ah! A Cat-house, I believe? How truly lupanarian and wonderful!" she said as he tried to hide his amazement that she already knew and had the cut of Mickey's jib. "Green doors, you say, boy? Was it not Pedro Calderón de la Barca who said that green is the prime colour of the world and that from which its loveliness arises?"

"I don't really know who that is or what you just said, Ma'am, but it did sound kinda cool. I'm glad I wasn't late." The driver looked puzzled. "Late, Ma'am. You said you insisted I wasn't late?"

She laughed like a little girl and said; "Oh! Sweet, wonderful you. I said the 'Sisters of Fate.' You know, the Moirai?"

He didn't and felt a bit silly, and yet, clearly, she didn't mind, and loved the innocence of youth. She squeezed his hand and smiled and the next period of silence was sheer, dream-like bliss.

Chapter Ten

Blackmail

Driving in Malta was dangerous and not fun, but with the absence of any rules, well, it turned out to be quite entertaining. As they steered through the narrow streets of the town, old ladies dressed wholly in black were crossing themselves as the vehicle passed and no doubt cursing the ungodly invaders. Gideon smiled at the two cultures and their differences.

The Maltese motorist hardly ever gave any signals and drove mainly in the middle of the road and sometimes you had to crawl behind them for ages as he indulged in excessive horn-hooting and weaving. Everything was allowed, apparently, and stupidity was forgiven, as long as you blew your horn! Welcome to Malta, and Gideon would not have wanted it any other way.

Gideon said to his glamorous driver, "Are they not supposed to drive on the left, Ma'am?"

She answered with a cute frown. "Supposed is not a word in the Maltese language young man, you will get used to it, trust me!"

As they drove up to a junction and stopped, an old Vauxhall taxi went straight through and Gideon thought why indeed, would a Maltese driver stop at an intersection? His vehicle backfired extremely loudly. Xanthe put her hands over her ears and said, "Mother of God that was calliopean!" He had never heard the word, but he knew what she meant from the context.

They drove on, the heat like a hairdryer in their faces. The Land Rover's air conditioning consisted of opening the two front vents and this just served to tunnel the hot blast and channel it all up their noses. She pulled the stick shift into fourth gear as they picked up speed and then put her hand on his inner thigh. "How do you feel?" she asked over the roar of the engine.

He paused and said truthfully, "Scared, surprised and overwhelmed. Happy too, though!"

"How refreshingly emotionally open you are. To quote the Greek philosopher, Epictetus, 'It's not what happens to you, but how you react to it that matters.'"

How wonderful. He had absolutely no idea what she had meant.

"This is of course the embodiment of his whole philosophy, that happiness is not defined by happy or sad things happening to us. It's our reactions and responses to events that that we can't control, and in your case, well, that's me!"

Gideon was amazed. Now, it sort of made sense?

"With that life philosophy in mind then, young man, achieving happiness becomes a much more tangible goal, the good Stoical man thought so, and I do also! Don't believe me? Well, you see this meeting as strange and unbelievable and yet, your response made it so, not me. You could have just said no, but being the sensitive and delightful soul I believe you are, you knew that if you didn't try this experience, then something would pass you by. Yes?" She didn't wait for his reaction. "Let me ask you this, then, are you happy to be here, right now, with me?"

"Yes Ma'am."

"And who walked off the gangway and turned right in response to my invitation?"

He was genuinely impressed with this explanation. Not knowing who Epictetus was didn't stop him from understanding this theory and he liked that very much.

"So, forget the mild discomfort and remember the experience. It's thoroughly appropriate and utterly delicious for me. Now then, what do you like to be called?"

Names had pigeonholes. A name like Quentin or Rupert or Nigel would be seen as upper-class. Working class sons would be Burt or Alfred or just Fred like their fathers, but Gideon thought his name was effeminate in the eyes of hardened seadogs – or anyone else for that that matter.

So he exhaled and spoke as his heart thumped. He said that he liked to be called 'Moo' but that he also very much liked the way she said agóri.

"Moo? As in bovine, as in the cow?" She laughed in surprise. "Were your parents mad?" she said, laughing harder now with one hand over her mouth. She loved the silliness of it all. Then, lowering her tone, she spoke seriously "My agóri, it translates as 'boy' in Greek," and she sang in her language as she drove with her white skirt hoisted up over her knees, showing a teasing amount of deeply tanned, olive-hued legs.

As they pulled up to her residence, known as the White Mansions, she cut the engine, which came to a clattering stop. She turned and looked very serious. "Tell me your real name just this once and I will never use it if that pleases you... agóri."

He felt at ease and said, "Gideon, Ma'am. Mickey thought it a bit strange and shortened it to Giddy."

He was surprised how comfortable he felt with this beautiful woman and as misty thoughts swirled through his head, she said, "I love it, Giddy. Now then, agóri, I want you to call me Xanthe, please."

"Yes, Ma'am" Gideon replied, then immediately realised what he had in fact called her.

"I have to get into mufti too. I'll not be long, I promise," she said as she disembarked and turned around and said with an incredible smile, "Agóri" and then scrunched up her nose and ran up the stairs and into the building without waiting for a reply. It was dawning on him that maybe this was a little more than a lift.

The White Mansions were an old building where the Wrens were billeted on the island. It was back around Valletta in a small district called Ta'Xbiex, the name coming from the Maltese for sunrise. The sun did indeed rise over Valletta and as it was on the eastern side of the island, it could be spectacular.

Xanthe had said that she had to see a superior about something relating to her Communication department, which she headed up, which meant nothing to the out-of-depth seaman. His head was full of conflicting things. He was off-duty and there was beer to be scuppered and ladies to dance with and regale with tales of fighting back evil boarders. But she was intoxicatingly beautiful, with a manner and demeanour he had only ever seen in movies he had sat watching alone in darkened rooms, dreaming of unattainable romance.

He thought of his mentor. Mickey would understand, wouldn't he? He would have waited too, he truly believed.

Officers don't date enlisted men. It's taboo. It's a court-martial offence. Moreover, he was only seventeen years old and although considered pretty by many and in very good shape, this woman was leagues above him in sophistication, knowledge and class. He clearly couldn't talk to her properly so why did he just roll over? Well, he was ordered to wasn't he? But he just wanted to be with her for as long as he could.

Pathetic he knew, but exciting too. Also, it didn't matter what he thought, as the lady wasn't in a million years giving him long-term consideration.

He had been involved with a well-educated girl back home, so he liked good English, but he had heard nothing as captivating as this. What made it different was that it was accessible to him. He didn't completely understand it, but he could guess, sort of, what this First Officer was saying about many things. He also found her language and intelligence embarrassingly arousing. He would soon learn that there was a word for this condition.

As he waited on those steps in the heat, his heart was thunderstruck. If he saw her just once more, then it would be enough. It was like looking at a handcrafted Aston Martin at a car show. One can look, one can smell, one can dream, but one will never touch, own, be with and cherish…?

"I need a drink!" said Xanthe as she came down the steps of the building an hour or so later, looking frustrated and upset. She was wearing a white dress with a screen-printed floral pattern and white sensible shoes. "Nuncheon!" she wailed, then she hoarsely whispered, "I'll show you a beguiling bar," as she drove past Marsamxett Harbour and along Tower Road, through St Julian's towards St Georges Bay in her beat-up old Ford. How very exotic this all was for Gideon and his thoughts were never further away from what had once been his home.

She was troubled about something service-related and wanted to blow a fuse away from the naval scenario. He told her that he absolutely loved her dress. She seemed to lighten up and looked genuinely flattered.

Gideon had only been in the Royal Navy for two years and at sea for just six months, but he had his feet firmly on the ground. He was just enjoying the moment. She said she would take him to a bar because she thought that's what he would like.

He did like, very much! He didn't ask what had made her so mad, but when in casual conversation he briefly mentioned Mr Hinkley, she said, "Ah, yes, that beastly Nigel!" He did not want to push it as it was none of his business. Sensing his discomfort, she said, "It's called blackmail." Then she dismissed the subject.

Chapter Eleven

The kiss

"So you told nobody of this meeting, then?" she said with concern. The street noises, with people shouting around them made it hard to hear.

He turned to her with longing and honesty and said, "Mickey knows, as you know, Ma'am, but he isn't a nobody to me."

She smiled and relaxed again and spoke so softly that he had to lean forward slightly. She touched his arm. "You trust him completely don't you? I love that in you. Beautiful boy."

"Please tell me, why you are angry?" Although in fact, her anger seemed to have gone.

"Mr Hinkley knows or rather suspects my feelings toward you, young sir. At cocktails last evening he cornered me and came right out with the notion that he now had the capability to ruin my career. Don't be concerned. I can handle that little weasel and for the first time that I can recall, I reminded him of my rank and position."

"Wow!" said Gideon. "He really is a shit... I mean, a horrible person, isn't he? You should hear what the boys say about him, Ma'am!"

"You are correct of course, sweet boy. And no, I don't think I would like to know what those pirates think. However, when I reminded him of our positions, you know, my standing, his rank and inexperience, he said, 'Well now, this doesn't seem to be the case under the circumstances, does it,' and it sent a chill down my spine. He loves prurient parlour games."

"I guess that makes him dangerous, doesn't it?"

"Dangerous? No. To be taken seriously and watched, yes. Leave it to me. You look lovely. And smell good too!"

They stopped on the way at St Julian's at a charming

hotel. There were many such quirky, old-fashioned establishments on the island. You never saw steel and glass constructions in Malta and every building was either old, ancient or scruffy. This one had been built on over the decades and the foyer had a black and white theme with columns up to a high ceiling. The many slow-moving ceiling fans, potted palms and old sofas in cosy alcoves made it look to Gideon like a movie set.

They walked in to the foyer where a waiter was waiting, and Xanthe ordered two ice-cold Dutch beers. "These are exciting times one feels," she said as she looked around, musing, "I'm not sure if the transition is going to be smooth from 1940s Catholicism to a neoteric state with all that inevitably comes with it."

"What does that mean, Ma'am, that word, neo something?"

"Well, inquisitive you, the Neoterics were the 'new poets': avant-garde Latin poets who wrote in the first century BC. Then the English language adapted the word from late Latin 'neotericus' which meant 'recent.' So anything neoteric is modern or new." Her eyes smiled at him. "I know that could seem a little pretentious but…"

Gideon stopped her with a gentle finger across those desirable lips. "Please go on… I don't really understand… and yet, I don't know why, but it sets me all buzzing."

"Well, well!" she said with warmth. "In my context, it means a modern and new dawn for this nation. And, the wonderful thing about this ancient word to me is that modern, the word that is, is itself, old." She shook her head like a schoolgirl and her eyes opened wide as if she had just found out there was chocolate in her lunch box, sneaked in by a loving parent.

In the space of four minutes he had not only learnt a new word, but had the root traced back through Latin and then applied to a burgeoning island race and a dying Empire. It was magical.

"I figure there is a Goddess for this right now isn't there, Ma'am?"

"How wonderful you would ask, pretty boy. Please call me Xanthe... and I choose Asteria, the Titaness Goddess of magic practices!" They had not even reached their seats.

They moved on quickly and arrived at a bar in St Georges Bay that was shabby and delightful in every way. The beaten up old Ford was left unlocked, which impressed Gideon, although he also wickedly thought: "Who would want to steal that shed anyway?" He laughed out loud and Xanthe looked at him lovingly and shook her head as though she knew precisely what he was thinking.

They had been together for just over an hour and they were already at ease with each other and his heart was racing with just that thought. What was happening to him?

The hotel faced the sea and there was a fabulous view from the bar with a veranda full of soft furnishings. As he stood there waiting for Xanthe to join him, he could smell the Mediterranean Sea air, which seemed to fill his whole being.

"Where are your thoughts?" Xanthe said from behind him, wrapping an arm around his waist.

"Well, it's different to anything I've seen. Tangier was extreme and Dorset is closed most of the time, but this place is so alive, isn't it?" He couldn't believe the feeling that her arm around his waist was giving him.

"Indeed it is, young sir. This is a mid-priced faded hotel which some would not think of coming to except those who care about ambiance and culture. Look at the view, what can you smell? Feel the soft faded leather and hear the chatter of the Maltese at leisure! Come on, isn't this special?"

It was true. The Maltese all looked busy doing nothing he thought with glee. How many times could that lovely grandma to the left of the veranda sweep the porch of the shop down below? What were those weather-beaten men talking about with such passion as they played their game of draughts, apparently with no intention of ever winning?

"Yes, and what was that word you used about this place earlier, *big* something or other?"

"Beguiling, my love. It means enchanting, often in a deceptive way." His mind was racing to put the word deceptive into her context, but then Xanthe said "Shushhhh," the most erotic sound ever, gently released from her mouth, which went on for nearly five seconds.

He sighed and asked her what she would like to drink.

"A large gin and tonic, unless you can tempt me with something equally desirable?"

Gideon said that she should try a John Collins made with Old Tom gin as it was a staple cocktail for sailors while in the Mediterranean. "Sometimes, it's called a Tom Collins too."

"Talk me through it!" she said, clasping her hands like someone in awe in front of a magician.

"Well its gin and lemon. A pinch of powdered sugar. The juice of half a lemon and a large shot of Old Tom gin. Shake up, or stir up with ice. A massive squirt from a soda siphon. Add a slice of lemon peel and add a dash of Angostura bitters to finish!"

"De rigueur for the zeitgeist?" Xanthe purred.

Gideon had absolutely no idea what she had said, but it made him glow. "My folks run an inn so I know that you wouldn't be able to tell what gin you were drinking once it was mixed. My father is a serious gin drinker. Old Tom gin is slightly sweeter than London Dry, but slightly drier than the Dutch Jenever. It works well with this cocktail."

"Well! I'll have what you're having," said the seraph, and he promptly ordered two.

They sat down on a sofa on that veranda. Gideon thought how his parents would be appalled at the idea of a sofa outside, which he liked very much indeed.

"Tell me about your folk then, young man. They run a pub you say?"

He was surprised by a sudden sadness and felt his whole demeanour change. He would never ask for sympathy on this subject. He didn't need any. But Xanthe looked at him and she seemed to see, and swiftly put her arm around his waist again. She pulled him close to her and moved her hand up his back and neck. Then she gently pulled his face to hers so that their lips met and in that first tender moment, their fate was sealed.

Chapter Twelve

The Bubble

"Where do you call home, Ma'am?" he said, still overly respectful. The memory of his parents had vanished – the only person who mattered was sitting right next to him.

"Wood Green in London," she laughed. "I am a Thessalonian from Thessaloniki, a fairly modern city on the Greek mainland. My parents were Greek but my mother fell in love with an English naval officer in Athens. He was an attaché there." She seemed passionate about her parents, although Gideon sensed an underlying sadness. "I was young at the time. My name went from Christodoulou to Craven and now, it reads "Yellow Yellow" firstly in Greek and then in English." She giggled at the silliness of it. "Xanthe means golden, you see, and craven means cowardly, or yellow!"

"Mickey said you were a Bubble to tease me, but what *is* a Bubble?"

Her face came alive, eyes eager. "How utterly charming that rakish fellow of yours is. It's cockney rhyming slang for Greek. 'Bubble and Squeak' – Greek. One only says the first word of the rhyme."

"Does one?" he mimicked her beautiful, upper-class received pronunciation and they smiled at each other.

She put her drink down and leaned over to kiss him again, softly. She picked his hand up and put it behind her neck and he was now able to pull her that tiny bit closer as if to take charge of this passionate, meaningful kiss, although there was no doubt who was responsible for this electric moment. The sun was still hot in the late afternoon and colourful boats bobbed in the harbour with their little flags flapping in the breeze. It was the most magical time and place.

As their lips parted, he wiped a tear from her cheek and

she whispered, "I know, I just know, beautiful you." He had absolutely no idea what she knew, but he knew that it would be life changing.

Xanthe signalled to the attentive barman and a waitress placed two more iced drinks on the table. She had never mentioned her age, but he figured that she was ten to twelve, maybe fifteen years older than him? It clearly didn't matter a jot to either of them. As Mickey had shown him at the top of Gibraltar, he was taking in every experience.

She really was impossibly beautiful. She had soft downy hair in front of her ears, which he found quite pleasing. He could imagine that she was a goddess, put on this mortal Earth to stupefy the male species. It was sure as hell working on Gideon.

As she talked, he discovered that their paths had crossed two or three times unbeknown to him in that first week, as he moved across the island, busy with the military withdrawal.

She said she had watched him when his working party had been at the Royal Naval Hospital Bighi, in Kalkara, helping a doctor who was prioritising equipment to be removed. Most of it would eventually stay, they all knew, but military rules had to be followed.

Xanthe spoke of a pretty Queen Alexandria nurse who had been flirting with him in an old theatre. Xanthe, the nurse's superior, had experienced a sudden frisson that went all the way down her spine.

He smiled and shook his head, and in perfect unison, they both said, "What's a frisson, Ma'am?" Their eyes burned into each other as they laughed.

"An immediate thrill, agóri. A sudden strong feeling, in my case, of excitement! Do you know of Athena, the goddess of wisdom?"

"The only Athena I know is a poster shop in England," he said. "Stop laughing at me!" But he was laughing at her laughter.

"Later, it is important. Anyway, I could see you were flattered with the pretty nurse's attention, but it was clearly not the time and place considering the little minx's superior was there – Miss Craven, the same lady now holding your arm."

"I love the way you talk, truly!" he said with as much passion that he could muster in his voice.

"Thank you. I watched that nurse and as she leaned forward to whisper encouragement in your ear, she touched your arm in a gesture of kindness, announcing her availability. I observed your bearing change dramatically at this small, powerful act, even though she did it to gain your attention, without any sincere affection."

He remembered. That nurse was of Indian heritage and reminded him of Jyoti. Xanthe was right, that touch had affected him.

He put his drink down and held both her hands. "Are we in trouble, Ma'am?"

"Are you the happiest you have ever been, agóri? Right here and now?"

"You know I am. I can tell you know!"

"Then let me say this. Epictetus said, 'Wealth consists not of having great possessions, but of having few wants.' These were his wonderful words. Want do you want? I want you. And be sure, I have never been with a man before. You are special to me. I am different. *We* are amazing."

The enormity of what she said set a new course on his journey. How could he walk back on board, shrug his shoulders and be casual and flippant after the last four hours? He looked into her dark, longing eyes and thought that his whole life had been worthwhile simply because it had led to this moment.

Xanthe had to leave at around six that evening for duty and she drove to the Triton Fountain, the meeting point for journeys across the island, to drop Gideon off. This circular 'square' was full of buses and people going everywhere and nowhere. The magnificent fountain dominated the centre and as he looked around, he could see parts of the old city walls with the magnificent gate looking through the passage to the heart of Valletta.

He understood why Xanthe had chosen this drop-off point. Nobody would pick them out here. The noise was amazing. This was the city's main bus terminal, and he could hear drivers arguing, vehicle horns and laughter.

He turned to face Xanthe and was going to mess this all up by saying something silly when she took charge. "Tomorrow, agápi mou, here, 1300 hours and don't be adrift, pretty boy!" He smiled with relief. What had she just said? Something Moo? She held him tightly. "Don't think this was a happy accident. I specifically asked to visit your ship for this to happen." She kissed him hard, held on to his shoulders and looked him in the eye.

"When I used the word the word *lupanarian* about that Green Door place, it was in envy and frustration. It means things connected to prostitution or sexual activity. I can take you higher than whatever they could do to you! We are already there, and here's the thing, you know it too! Now, off you go and be yourself, not a paradigm of how people see foreign sailors."

She drove off through the madness of the city and he smiled at her jalopy clattering away.

Chapter Thirteen

Pandora's box

Strait Street was easy to find, as was Mickey. He had a voluptuous lady on his lap and gently sat her down and walked towards the bar to speak to Gideon. "Jesus son, look at you, all lit up like a beacon! Tell me what happened, then?"

"She was kind and funny and very interesting. Very clever too without being showy or lecturing. And she has ordered me to be at the Triton tomorrow at 1300. What does Athena mean to you, Mick?"

"Fucking poster shop, innit?"

Gideon should have seen that coming. "But was there a Greek goddess called Athena?"

"Fuck knows, Gids, there was hundreds of those weirdos, make no mistake. Why do you ask?"

"She wants to talk to me about her, Athena that is. Thought I'd find out a bit about her first."

"Ask the Navigating Officer, he's into all that bollocks. Now let's have a gallon of beer and you can tell me more, then we'll have a quick jump on one of these lovely-smelling ladies!"

"Beer... yes, please! Ladies – not today, thanks. She said something about a paradigm. I don't know what that is, but the way she said it, I know she didn't want me to do that. Something has happened to me, Mick."

"I respect that, Giddy. Don't understand it, but if I had a woman like that, I think I'd be the same. Where do you think this is going to end, though?"

Gideon felt crushed suddenly. Why did he think it was going to end?

The sailors had an amazing time in Strait Street: everything was raucous and funny, and just stumbling back for the water taxis was entertaining in itself. But later,

Gideon took ages to get to sleep, thinking about what had happened to him that day.

He met Xanthe for the second time the next day at 1300 as requested, so this was effectively, their first real date. Gideon slipped ashore alone at midday, caught a *dghajsa* and walked to the Triton Fountain. He stood there for what seemed like an age, but was very comfortable in the bustling environment. He had been briefed that this was one of the safest places in the world and he felt that amongst the hundreds of Maltese folk milling around him.

He tried to look cool and unemotional, but his heart was racing with anticipation when suddenly, a soft voice from behind him said, "I am looking for a boy to change my life." He swirled around and was about to speak when she said, "You look like a boy who cares. I like that very much indeed." She kissed him passionately.

She took his hand and they made their way to her car, which was parked a short distance away at the Phoenicia Hotel.

As they drove up towards Sliema, Gideon thought how alive and glowing she was, and she kept touching him, as often as her concentration allowed her. He loved the hot, dusty air blowing through every window in this rickety but reliable vehicle.

As they stopped at a traffic hold-up, Xanthe turned to him with a gentle and meaningful tone, "Look me in the eye, young man! I mean it agóri, my life starts here. I have wanted you from that first moment in Lascaris. We cleaved. I came on board your vessel and made this happen." Something was very different about her today. Still amazing, but with a new enthusiasm.

"You know what I like about you?" she said. "Like Socrates, you know just how much you don't know! And you have an unpretentious honesty, but also a vain attitude of overconfidence, which of course the Navy embraces too." Gideon didn't know much about Socrates, but he did know he was something to do with wisdom. And his father had always thought he was an idiot!

They couldn't move because a donkey was refusing to budge, and people were driving over the pavement, endangering flower pots, bicycles and pedestrians in order to get around it.

As they finally moved off she continued, "You completed the long months' training and sub-specialised branch and here you are doing a man's job for a man's pay. Britain is not playing at this and neither am I, beautiful boy!"

"So… you said we cleaved?" he said in a gentle mocking tone, which he could tell she liked.

"Yes, it's really important that you asked. It means to be emotionally attached to someone, deeply involved, and to resist separation. I knew this as soon as our eyes met in the Comcen. You knew it too." She looked at him and smiled. "To cleave. It's an intransitive verb. And a homograph, too!" She clearly loved his curiosity about language, but Gideon knew that she had said that last bit to tease him. "Love at first sight if you like," she added. He had not seen that coming.

As they drove closer to their destination, she talked about his gentle demeanour, unassuming nature and burgeoning maturity, and how all this had made him more than attractive to her. She spoke of the swaggering Jolly Jack Tar of folklore and said, "My goodness me, there are plenty of those fabulous characters onboard the Euryalus, colouring the world with salty anecdotes and sightings of mermaids, aren't there?"

Gideon smiled at all his newfound knowledge and at the thought that they had cleaved.

They had the most wonderful hour drinking cocktails in another second-rate hotel, but later the bar began to fill up with service personnel in mufti and so they slipped away and escaped to a waterfront bar in Sliema.

They talked and talked with fresh enthusiasm. Her cool, husky assurance, albeit with a giggly, girlish edge, was calming for him and her constant touching was pleasing beyond anything that had ever happened to him.

She wanted a weekend away, which was like saying, 'Let's not only play with fire, let's hold on to the burning end.' This part of the conversation brought him back to Earth.

"We must get away. Just request a weekend off, agápi mou, a seventy-two hour pass. I will arrange for you to observe my friends who are doing archaeological work on Gozo! Does it not say in your BR 1938 handbook that a young sailor should, and I quote: 'Take an intelligent interest and play his full part in all activities of a ship's daily life.' One can interpret this in many ways, don't you think? And, simply because we're abroad, an observation of this kind can definitely be seen as an intelligent interest."

He hadn't read BR 1938 lately, even though it was issued to every recruit on entry. He understood her argument but was still concerned.

"Take a chance!" she said. "Here are the rules: 'Ignore the rules.' It's a well-known paradox and it's applicable here."

"Paradox!" Gideon said suddenly. "I know her! She had a box that she shouldn't have opened, didn't she?" Her wide-eyed laughter as she explained his mistake made him fall a little bit more in love with her.

The afternoon turned to early evening and she had to go back on duty. Gideon wondered what he would do without her. At least he knew who Pandora was now.

Chapter Fourteen

Edith Swan-neck.

On board the next morning, he submitted a request form for weekend leave and although usually this was a perfectly reasonable action, it was frowned upon for one so young in a foreign land.

Mickey went to see the Master-at-Arms and explained Gideon's love of history and that he would be well looked after by the archaeology team, who they had met at the hospital whilst in a working party, which was true. They had stumbled across the group in the hospital in Kalkara, and now it turned out that they were friends of Xanthe. Mickey stuck his chest out and explained in an earnest fashion that Gideon had the chance to be educated and he would come back on Tuesday morning a changed man after the experience of a lifetime!

Some were concerned that Gideon was acting strangely, but they let it go. The day-to-day life of service personnel had been turned upside-down by the withdrawal operation, and many unusual situations were deemed normal in the chaos.

Gideon knew that Mickey was aware of his precarious situation and would have his back. Often the pair would go ashore together and meet Xanthe somewhere deserted, and when contact was made, he would bow, kiss her hand and request that she look after the boy, saying, 'Ma'am' and all that subservient stuff before he shot off and left them alone. Xanthe loved all this.

An extended seventy-two hour weekend pass was granted to Gideon without any fuss.

That Friday afternoon, Mickey and Gideon walked to the bustling bus terminus at the fountain. They met up with 'the Raven,' Mickey's new code for her, who was waiting for them in a beat-up old white Ford Anglia covered in dust and driven by her friend, Melanie. Melanie was stationed in St Angelo and was billeted some distance from the White Mansions.

Xanthe was wearing a voguish, full white tailored dress, which parodied her uniform. It left little to the imagination and showed off her wasp-like waist and voluptuous breasts. A visible panty line was a sin in Malta and she was showing one for all to gape at. The outfit was completed by a silver necklace with a Greek key design around her smooth, swan-like neck. As Gideon leaned forward to kiss that neck, the aroma of patchouli overpowered him and he remembered where he had smelled it before.

The plan was to head north on a bus. These were family-run 'char-à-bancs' which were the pride of the owner-operators with their images of the Virgin Mary and Jesus, rosary beads and nick-knacks clacking, hanging, stuck to and wrapped around everything. The vehicles were predominately yellow, although there were green and red ones too, but all were bedecked with this religious paraphernalia. It was unique, quaint and quintessentially Maltese.

Most of the drivers were rotund and had moustaches, and all were incredibly happy and friendly. They were so pleased that you were getting on *their* bus and not their cousin Gorg's or Uncle Joseph's and their pride made this experience their mission. A bus timetable was nowhere to be seen. You just asked a driver if he was heading north and if wasn't, he'd point you to the bus that was. It worked like a dream.

"*Omnia Audax* my young friends, *Omnia Audax*," Mickey said, bowing and backing off smiling as they boarded and Gideon turned to look at him perplexed and slightly annoyed.

She would know, wouldn't she, he thought as they drove off through the bustling, dusty streets. "What does that mean, Ma'am?" he asked as they headed northwest.

"*Daring in all things* if my Latin serves me still," she said.

70

"You knew that?!" he said.

She smiled. "No, but I made it my business to find out!"

Of course she did, he thought. That's why she was so unbelievably smart and fascinating. He was, momentarily, angry with his parents for not supervising his education closely enough, but the feeling soon passed.

Mickey had known all along what the motto meant! Or maybe he had asked someone about it more recently? Gideon shook his head in bewilderment and awe for these two warriors of the world who were special to him in very different ways.

She was talking and he was immediately attentive. "Please call me Xanthe, will you? I love the way you say Ma'am, but you don't have to when we are alone." He couldn't say anything then, which wasn't like him. She said reassuringly, "It's alright, lovely you, it will come naturally. You will know when it is right!"

Gravitino, the friendly bus driver, was in full Maltese mode as he pulled away, insulting every other driver and most pedestrians, blowing his horn, crossing himself and telling folk that their mothers were porcine incarnations of the Devil and would burn in hell!

That journey north was his first proper foreign trip as an adult. "Think Odyssey," she whispered, reading his thoughts as she cupped his chin in her hand, and then kissed the tip of his nose and his lips. "This sedate Isle of Gozo, our destination, is said to have been the home of the mythological Calypso, the nymph who imprisoned Odysseus. Homer's *Odyssey* is the story of his journey back after the Trojan Wars." He knew nothing of this myth but felt that he loved it already.

As they took the twenty-five-minute ferry ride over to Gozo, their mood softened after that dusty, barren drive north to the terminal. The warm, southerly, hair-dryer-like Sirocco wind from within the continent now mixed with a local wind as it swept up over Tunisia. She told him that it was known as 'the Chili' and as it moved north over the archipelago, it revitalised their mood.

"Purging and purifying," she said, "cleansing, releasing, freeing, exorcising, it all adds up to one word, *cathartic*." She swirled around like a girl in a playground. "I want to teach you about Aeolus, the Greek keeper of the winds." Gideon couldn't wait.

On the ferry, there were two families, clearly related, and they were arguing as only the Maltese could, it appeared to Gideon. "I can't believe how passionate they are when they're shouting at each other," he said.

"No my love, they are not shouting, they are arguing with slightly raised voices." He could see that now and his thoughts drifted back to his former home and the pain that stemmed from alcohol and hate. This was so different.

Xanthe started to talk about how different peoples argued. "The Spanish seem to be the most proficient, followed by the Italians and the Greeks! But lowly English insults are impressive too."

"Why do you say that, Ma'am?"

"Well, I have an abhorrence of ignorance and I do not think it correct to talk about Mr Hinkley at this juncture, but I note that in conversation with me you called him a moron. Am I correct?"

"Yes, I did!"

"Quite right, too. You should know, agápi mou, idiots were, a long time ago, those whose mental development never exceeded that of a child of two. Please, don't think of your impudent father and what he said. Imbeciles were those whose development was higher than that of an idiot, but whose intelligence did not exceed that of a child of seven."

Gideon loved this. "And…" she drew this out, "morons were those whose mental development was above that of an imbecile but did not exceed that of a child of twelve. It's an outdated thought, but it puts things into perspective, don't you think?"

"So Mr Hinkley really *is* a moron!"

They held on to each other and laughed. He loved it that Xanthe could use words like *impudent* when she talked of his father. And that he now knew what 'idiot' really meant and his father did not.

"What does Michael call me?" Xanthe asked. The wind made her hair blow wildly around her head like something in a dream. He loved the way she called Mickey 'Michael,' it was so bloody upper-class and sexy.

"Craven the Raven."

"Ah! Craven the Raven who is unshaven and some say, a maven?" He felt a pang in his nether regions. "Can he be trusted to be discreet?"

"He's all the family I really have..." He tailed off as he could not find the words to explain. She gently covered his hand with hers. He trusted Mickey and she trusted him.

Gideon wasn't at all religious, but he found himself bastardising a quote that he had read or heard and said aloud: "And then God said, let there be light, and beauty… so he made Greek women!"

"You have the most swan-like neck," he added.

"Nobody has ever said that before. Why do you say it with such a sparkle in your eye?"

Gideon loved the chance to explain. "My favourite English king is Edward III, but a close second would be Harold, as in 1066 and all that. He had a lover called Edith Swan-Neck and she was recorded as walking through a field full of dead bodies after the battle of Hastings, trying to find Harold's body parts, as only she could identify him by certain blemishes and other features. Honestly, I read about it!" he said earnestly. "I've always loved that fact and think about it when I read English history. Harold came to the Abbey at Cerne Abbas, which is only four miles from my village back in England. His mother was the Abbess there, so I figure Edith was there at some stage too. And Edith is one of my favourite female names."

"What an utterly delicious story," she said, flicking the overabundant hair away from the left side of his head, up and over his ear. This made him all-a-quiver and he held her warmly and kissed her very gently on the forehead, and then that Greek nose of hers and then down to those bee-sting, maroon-coloured lips. She tasted salty from the spindrift and for a moment there were no words.

"And you think of your Edith when you look at my neck? I have a long neck. It's what helps make me five foot nine!"

"No, I think Edith had a neck like yours. You are my Edith."

It came out all wrong and silly, but she didn't seem to think so. She squeezed his upper arms with a sigh and a little gasp and said, "You don't know what you do to me, agápi mou. I have never had such feelings with a man."

Chapter Fifteen

Boy to man

And so the ferry berthed on the island of Gozo. If Malta was twenty years behind England, then Gozo was fifty years behind.

"The island is oval-shaped and it's twenty-six square miles in size, approximately the same area as New York's Manhattan Island. Although I know the English prefer to use football pitches as a measurement…" Xanthe said.

"And Wales, Ma'am!" he said. Xanthe looked confused. "Wales is a measurement in England too. You know Australian bush fire the size of Wales is out of control somewhere in Didgery-Poo's town…"

She smiled, and Gideon watched as she walked across the deck and wandered to the guardrail to inhale the air. He tried to fathom what was different about her today. She just glowed. She had slipped off her rope sandals and strung them onto her bag. She turned and spoke softly, "Going barefoot is totally acceptable on these islands. 'Discalced' is the word for it, if you were wondering! It comes from a rigorous order of Catholic nuns and Friars who go barefoot."

How more desirable could a woman look and smell and be? He held her shoulders from behind and inhaled her essence.

Everything on Gozo was shades of brown from deep to sand-coloured. There was no greenery anywhere except for an odd-looking tree that looked like a larger bonsai tree that had survived under extraordinary hardship.

They disembarked and Xanthe was twisting her hair with her finger and was stroking her neck with a pleased expression. "Gozo, we think, comes from the Greek 'gaudos,' which is derived in turn from the Phoenician word for a small boat. The Greeks did not actually colonise these islands, but had a strong influence over their history. One can find many inscriptions and there have been coins found that suggest that we were here between the 6th and 7th centuries."

"How do you know all this?" he said with warmth.

"I lived here as a little girl for two years. Come, let's get this taxi!"

A cream-coloured old taxi waited just down the jetty and the driver, who was wearing a Breton cap at a jaunty angle, urged them towards it. "It's a 1954 Vauxhall Cresta E," he pronounced proudly as he drove north. Their destination was a villa that she owned jointly with her brother. It faced east on the East Coast in a time-stood-still, forgotten place called Marsalforn.

Gideon smiled. "Do you know what the E stands for?" The driver didn't. "I believe it stands for 'Executive,' Sir." Gideon told him.

This newfound knowledge changed the driver's facial expression. "Very much thank you, my friend!" he said and the journey from then on was wonderful because of his blissful, toothless smile in the rear-view mirror.

It was lovely to feel that they had stepped back in time, and all three people seemed to be in harmony with the landscape and life, and this marvellous piece of British engineering from Luton, Bedfordshire.

They pulled up to a row of eight or ten old villas, all in varying degrees of repair. There were many little flat-roofed houses in the rocky pink and ochre landscape and a few dotted behind which gave the place a Biblical feel against a serene and barren background. The villa they arrived at looked like a huge cooking pot and was the first round building Gideon had seen anywhere on these islands.

"The last time I saw a house like this, my sister was playing in it. It was Noddy's house!" he said, loving the villa's quaintness. It looked basic and undeveloped, but Gideon thought, why would you change perfection? Its simplicity took his breath away, and the quiet there was unbelievable, with only the odd puff of wind to let him know that he was still on Earth.

They gazed at a wonderful view. She told him that 'marsa' was Arabic for port or bay. The magical, multi-coloured fishing boats were called 'luzzu,' and their design dated back to Phoenician times. Dozens of them bobbed in the little cobalt-blue harbour.

As the taxi driver drove away, he waved and said from his window; "You folk have many chil-dred!" and they both smiled. Xanthe had handed him a small sum of money, amounting to about a month's wages on the island.

Inside, the villa was a little rundown in a romantic way, with distressed wooden furniture and simple fittings and of course, the ever-present wooden depiction of the Virgin Mary on the white-washed wall. Everything to Gideon looked very Greek.

Xanthe said, "This is what life means, agápi mou. Meeting folk, talking, learning and experiencing… giving." She made a sweeping gesture of her arm and whispered, "Many chil-dred!"

Gideon laughed. "I loved his vehicle. I mean, really. I have childhood memories of a car like that, and his enthusiasm was just wonderful to see. Melanie's Ford Anglia had that effect on me too!"

"Yes, and you were so kind and gentle. This is so important. I love this about you, very much. Does it really mean Executive? The 'E' I mean?"

"Not really," he said, "I was making it up on the spot. It might mean that, but I genuinely don't know." She kissed him hard. And then harder.

The villa had a pretty, xeriscape garden, which she said needed little watering or maintenance. Gideon could smell the aroma of its flora as it mingled with the salty air.

"It was my stepfather's garden," she said with casual pride. "He always kept a boat down there too, in the bay! This was all bequeathed to my brother, Tomaso, and me."

Xanthe's stepfather, the English officer, had been based there for twenty-four months and that was when he had purchased the property from a local government official for around four hundred English pounds, a lot of money in 1955.

Xanthe spoke with enthusiastic glee about the weekend ahead and said that they also had the use of a Citroen that was garaged and maintained by a local man called Mr Zammit. Her stepfather had employed him from time to time and he was still the caretaker of the villa when it was empty.

"Can I have a quick look, please?" he asked, intrigued by the idea of the car.

"For sure, Mr Curious, it's in the shack behind the pool. The key is by the door."

The key to the shack was indeed by the kitchen door and it was like the ones Gideon had seen in black and white horror movies: four inches long, big, cumbersome and made of solid iron. Unlocking the shack door was like opening an old castle: the door creaked and swung open and in the poor light, Gideon could already see that the vehicle was something unique. Two chrome headlights glared at him and a sizeable vertical grille had two arrowhead chevrons on it. Gideon became breathless as he realised it was a 1934 Citroen Traction Type 7A, aubergine, with black wheel arches. It looked beautiful and alien in the shadows. The paintwork, he thought, was the colour of her lips.

He walked back up to the villa and closed the door quietly. Xanthe was standing there in the narrow hallway with a glass of wine, wearing a Panama hat, a coy smile showing her sparkling white teeth.

"How say you, boy?"

She looked like an unattainable actress from a dream sequence or a fantasy fairy-tale. That hat just ticked the last box for perfection. She seemed to see that he didn't know what to say to make sense of the moment, so she took her hat off and put it on a worn wooden ledge just inside the front door. She pulled out the silver sword from her Greek hair clasp and let her hair cascade down. Then she leaned her backside on the ledge and beckoned him over.

"Kiss me, slowly please," she whispered.

He thought his chest was going to explode with the raw animalism of the moment. He hadn't been allowed to kiss that woman in Morocco, but now this lovely Greek demanded it. How he adored her aubergine lipstick – it transformed her olive beauty and as she bit her lip, there was no doubt who was in total control.

She pulled the soft Egyptian cotton of her dress gently up over her thighs and now sat on that wooden altar of love and slid out of her white lace panties. She pulled Gideon towards her and held that aromatic underwear right under his nose before letting it drop silently to the stone floor. Then she put her Panama hat back on, all her lustrous hair tumbling down over her shoulders.

She whispered in his ear, "*Festina lente,*" then gently explained, "Make haste slowly, agápi mou."

Standing there in awe, he thought he would explode like a schoolboy, but dared to look down at her. He had not seen anything like this before: the jet-black, shiny, soft hair overflowed in a single line up to her navel and down to the most delicate part of her inner thighs. He could not move for a moment at the sight of her beautiful protruding pubic bone, but he needed to move. He pulled off his shorts.

She inserted her middle finger through that triangular black forest and gently rubbed herself three or four times and this caress drove her chin upwards and caused her back to arch. She let out a euphonious moan that shook Gideon to the core. She then held him and guided him inside her and whispered. "No man has ever been here, my beautiful boy."

The sensation was intense as she put her hands on his shoulders and leaned back to look at his expression and the co-joining of their bodies.

"Look down, lover," she whispered and as he did, she pulled him from her and rubbed the tip of his penis up and over her clitoris eight, ten, twelve times, before she inserted it back inside of that field of dreams. Then she threw her head back and screamed with ecstasy as they detonated together. "Don't move," she quivered. "Don't ever move darling, please!"

Her legs were wrapped around him and her nails dug into the flesh at the back of his neck as she kissed him hard she cried, "We will never be apart, now! You are my *desiderata*! I love you!"

Chapter Sixteen

The Humming Chorus

After many minutes just holding each other, Xanthe pushed his chin up with one finger and said "Beer!"

They untangled and she held his hand and walked him through to the kitchen and sat him down at the table. She opened two ice-cold Dutch beers by smashing the tops off on the edge of the table. It was the most unladylike thing she had done in front of him and yet, it was the coolest thing he had ever seen.

"I love your whole… thing!" he said in admiration.

She said with glee, "I believe you mean to say *aura* in place of that cheeky little word, 'thing?' It is something that metaphorically radiates from a living creature, in this case, me, and it's regarded as an essential part of the individual."

After the beer she opened a bottle of wine and led him to the bedroom. They lay on the creaky old bed, entwined and drinking the wine. This was a new taste to Gideon, acidic and fruity. He could not take his eyes off her bare stomach.

Xanthe put her glass down and cupped her intimate part. She told him that the female pubic bone is covered by the urethral sponge: a layer of fat forming the mons pubis. She toured her femininity for him and never once laughed, teased or made him feel foolish in his fledgling state.

The initial sexual act between the two was short because of his inexperience, but bewitching and heavenly too with her guidance and understanding. He felt that he was changing right there and then from the schoolboy who had left England not so very long ago.

She said, "That was wonderful, my love. It was ephemeral and lasted just the right time, but now we must make love, deeply and passionately." They connected again and might have flown into another universe.

After a metamorphic hour or so, Gideon got up to use the

toilet and on the way back, he stared out to sea as the wind whistled a tune. Xanthe shimmied silently up to him from behind and he could feel her protruding pubic hair on his naked rump and those warm, soft breasts on his back. As she wrapped her arms around him she whispered, "Listen to the susurrus... that whispering, murmuring, rustling sound. Can you not hear Aeolus, the keeper of the winds?"

His mind raced at the notion that there was a Greek god controlling this wind. After turning him around, she kissed his untrained, adolescent mouth and said: "And what you are feeling is ataraxia, darling... it means equanimity and tranquillity of the mind!" She pulled her silk kimono on. "I want to talk to you soon about that Greek keeper of the winds, Aeolus. But that can wait. More wine!"

The subjects Xanthe talked about seemed essential to him now and he wondered why this stuff wasn't taught at school? She had such insight and could analyse people and understand any given situation accurately, rapidly and of course, with her exceptional talent, intelligently. Her passion for all this made her even more beautiful to him.

"I see your education and the lack of parental love has affected you,' she said now. "You simply must turn this into a strength. I believe you are finding your own way now, and the Service is guiding you and how wonderfully you are responding, agápi mou."

"My parents have managed to get my brother on the Euryalus," he confided. "It's driving me nuts, I don't know why..."

Xanthe gently put her arms around him as he ran out of words. "How sweet! Should I meet him? Would that help you?"

"No Ma'am, I wouldn't want any of my family to tarnish this. He's really alright, but not very bright. He might make fun of you, you know, all that blokes' stuff. We're not close. Xanthe, what's that Greek phrase you keep saying to me please? Something Moo?"

"Agápi mou? It means my love."

"I love the way you say it, with your native accent."

"And I love you. Truly!" she said and put on a heavy Greek accent as they entwined.

They were brought back to earth by a timid knock on the door. "Ah! The provender!" Xanthe said.

Without being visibly concerned, she walked to the bedroom, threw a sweater on and skipped to the creaky front door, gently stroking Gideon's cheek as she passed. She started speaking a language he could not understand and collected a cardboard box with a cloth over it. The small clay oven had been lit before they arrived and there was wine in a fridge that would not look out of place in a 1950s American domestic kitchen. Mr Zammit was indeed a dutiful and excellent person.

"You have been to Morocco, agóri, what did you like to eat there?"

He could not remember much: some kind of stew for sure and the kebabs undeniably, but they had mainly eaten onboard.

"Hmm, I figured as much, but I have a treat for you this evening! Have you heard of Maghreb cuisine?" Of course, he had not. "Well, it's food from the whole of the Arab part of North Africa, including Morocco. They use pigeon a lot for this dish, but I have had it made with chicken." She let him see and smell the box that had been delivered. Inside was a huge pie. "Apricots too!" she said with pride.

He thought of Mickey saying that the 'rag-heads' in North Africa were Arabs; and now her explanation of the word *Maghreb*. I love you Mickey he thought, but I'm leaning towards Xanthe's view of that part of the world!

"What's that overpowering aroma?" he said.

"That will be the combination of spices: cinnamon and lots of it, ginger especially and I couldn't get hold of saffron so had extra cumin sprinkled over it instead. It is called a Berber pasty, Mr Dorset, an object close to your heart, I'll bet!"

"Really? A Berber pasty?" he said, delighted. She held his neck and put her other hand across his mouth to shush him. "No, silly, I'm teasing. It is a Moroccan dish that uses a pastry the chef couldn't find, so he used filo dough instead and as a starter, my favourite Greek dish, spanakopita!" She had said this last word in that mock Greek accent again. "Say it with me agóri; spanakopita! If you have not tried spanakopita before, then you're in for a surprise, Mr meat-eater extraordinaire. It's a delicious savoury Greek pie made of perfectly crispy layers of filo dough and a comforting filling of spinach and feta and ricotta cheese. The filling also has fresh parsley, dill, garlic, eggs, onions, olive oil, salt and pepper. The Greeks like it with honey or Maple syrup, but I like it with cracked black pepper-corns: cold, simple and oh! So Hellenic!"

She made it sound so wonderful that his heart soared. Life with her was just so extraordinary.

"You know of a Moroccan chef? Here? And you speak Arabic? Why am I not surprised?"

She laughed. "I do speak Arabic and bizarrely, he has Moroccan in him, but he is actually a Maltese who speaks Greek!"

Spanakopita would be his favourite non-meat dish from that moment on.

After dinner, she put some long-playing vinyl on the gramophone and a melancholic voice pleaded with them in a language he couldn't understand, but he felt that soprano's need and her pain. So many things were thrilling his senses for the first time as if he had just been born an adult.

"Do you know what she is saying?" Xanthe asked, head to one side, hands clasped together.

"Not a word," said Gideon. "But I seem to get what she means…"

"That's because it is so, so powerful. I call it auditory velvet. This style of music has been an abiding force in my life since I first heard it played by my stepfather on this gramophone. I have always wanted to be able to share my love for this genre."

The track was *'O Mio Babbino Caro'* and Xanthe said, "I think it would be fair to say it's Pavlovian for me to hear those crackles."

She walked over to the gramophone and selected another long-playing disc. Gideon saw a Geisha lady on the colourful sleeve. She put the record on and placed the stylus some three quarters of the way across it. It crackled mellifluously. She walked over to him and put a scented hand across his mouth again. "This is *'Coro a bocca chiusa'* or 'chorus with mouth closed.' Please don't speak for the next three minutes."

The choir started to hum and he was overwhelmed with the sadness and grief, without really knowing why. He couldn't take his eyes off Xanthe as she kept her hand over his mouth for the entire three minute performance. The voices hummed through chords that he had never realised could sound so powerful – they pierced his soul and Gideon would never be able to hear that piece again without tears in his eyes.

He started to move his head from side to side slowly, and she whispered, "It makes me already miss things that haven't happened to us yet, Gideon! That was the Humming Chorus from the opera Madam Butterfly. As it diminuendos, listen to that ethereal B flat major chord!" The B flat, whilst piercing his heart, meant nothing to him. He wanted more of this. Much, more. Why did he know so little?

As she took her hand away from his mouth, she moved it like a conductor, her long finger going down with a swirling motion. As if in response, the humming grew quieter and in a pure and perfect moment, fell silent.

Chapter Seventeen

Education

Xanthe led him to the patio with its small swimming pool and poured more wine. She said that to open up your soul, you must listen to sad music. "There is a famous quote that says, 'Music sounds the way emotions feel.' That's what you have just experienced, my love."

Goodness, he had experienced that indeed. It was a perfect setting as they were not overlooked and the villa blocked the sometimes mean Eastern wind, although in that day's heat, it would have been most welcome.

"The child in the opera is called Dolore. It means sorrow. He is born under extraordinary circumstances of unrequited love. I abhor the word unrequited. It always makes me want to cry, even though it's fiction."

Beads of perspiration were running down her neck. He wanted to lick the droplets up with his tongue and drink her cast-off waste.

"Unrequited?" he said, already slightly saddened by this word.

"It was not returned. She loved him, but he did not love her back. A common enough scene in real life and devastating in this opera."

Gideon had, as Mickey advised, talked to the Navigating Officer of the Euryalus and asked about the goddess Athena.

He said now to Xanthe, with love and understanding, "The Navigating Officer on board told me that Athena remained a virgin, but had incredible close relationships with women too. Would that be you, beautiful lady?"

"If that were to be the case, what would your reaction be?" she said, apparently caught off balance.

"Totally acceptable on every level, Ma'am." He told her about his introduction to the story of Nisus and Euryalus and how he couldn't believe it initially. "It's not me, but if you love someone, I guess it just has to be?"

"Madam Butterfly's Humming Chorus brings on synaesthesia for me, agápi mou." She glanced at him and he looked back, open and ready to learn. Gosh, how he was learning. "It's a condition where one sense of the body stimulates another. Some people hear music and see it as colours. For me, that chorus pierces my heart and unlocks my tear ducts. Synaesthesia. See?" He did. He truly did. Not just the word itself but that the music reminded her of a woman, perhaps one she had loved.

"But now I've finally met someone who finds the same beauty in this opera as I do. This piece perfectly captures the feeling that one is willing to risk almost anything for one person. I love you so very much, Gideon. Yes, there was a woman, but my synaesthesia is for you. I have for the first time fallen in love. Not just lust, not the fascination I have experienced with women. True love, Gideon!"

The use of his name jolted him and she hugged him like the world was going to end. She whispered some words in her native language that he neither understood nor needed to, as her eyes said everything.

As she prepared dinner in the kitchen, he lay there by the pool and his thoughts were buzzing with Xanthe's aura. Yes, his heart now had a purpose and there she was humming in the kitchen and looking radiant, but the overriding thought in his mind was how all this new knowledge had changed his outlook. One word could devastate, another could induce tears, and chords in music could make your stomach churn or your heart leap.

After lunch Xanthe and Gideon were lying back by the pool and she was reading a German philosopher called Nietzsche. She showed an image of him and Gideon thought he looked totally insane. Still, when she quoted from that book, he loved it and it made sense. Like the modern magazines, Xanthe only read the best bits so that eventually, she hoped, he might read the book himself. He thought he might, although if she had just given him the book right off the bat, he would have been bogged down with the heavy text.

"You know, Nietzsche went mad in the end," she added.

"I could tell!" he said, delighted that his initial diagnosis had been right.

Xanthe suddenly put her book down, swung her legs over the lounger and sat up. She held both arms out and he walked towards her and took those hands as he knelt.

She spoke seriously, looking him in the eye. "If you were wondering why this is happening, try not to demystify it or compare the attraction of the physical to the craving and passion of one's soul."

They kissed hard and he bit her on the shoulder gently. He wanted to eat her up, she was so delicious. She seemed to love the initial shock of the pain and then his immediate release so as not to hurt her, and they looked into each other's eyes. Why were her eyes so amazing, he thought, and his were just an inferior sort of green? She got up to use the bathroom and he stepped into the azure-tiled pool to calm his lustfulness. Could life be any better? Could he ever be so happy again?

Not a chance he thought, with a boyish grin.

Later, Gideon was toking on a cold beer and thinking about their conversation. He looked at her lovingly, his libido stirring and without lifting her sunglasses or even moving her head, she said: "Are you thinking I'm esculent, you naughty boy?"

"Yes!" he said, not knowing the word.

His anticipation of her explanation made him hot-blooded and he waited with a pounding heart for this husky-voiced angel of enlightenment to sweep him away once more. He wasn't ready for what she said next, though.

"It means good enough to eat," she said and with that, she slowly lifted one leg over the side of the sun-lounger to show the most anticipated port of call any man could visit.

This would remain the finest example of how education is passed on by a wise teacher to a raw pupil: the brain is introduced to the theory, and then a practical demonstration ensures that the knowledge stays with the disciple forever.

She slid her middle finger deep down inside to make ready the harbour for an eager ship to dock inside her. But first, he must eat. He had been told to do so!

Chapter Eighteen

Hoka-Hey!

After an hour's sleep, the evening was upon them and they bathed together under a cold shower. The header tank was filled from a well and Gideon wasn't sure how all that worked.

Gideon was watching her later as dusk darkened her olive skin. She was wearing a light, flowing white dress and as he looked at her magnificent profile listening with her eyes closed to Puccini's 'Signore Ascolta,' he thought that this was a powerful and potent cocktail of how a woman should be. An incredible calm overcame him. He knew that he had fallen for her beyond reasoning.

As the soprano finished her angst, Xanthe got up, walked silently around the table, wrapped her perfume-scented scarf around his neck and pulled him towards her. "Tell me the word you're trying to think of," she said.

"Well, your womanishness..." He could not finish his sentence.

"Deal, young man. If you can remember my name, I'll tell you a wonderful word that describes a woman and all her femininity."

His hand cupped her neck and his thumb stroked the downy hair he liked so very much, as he watched a tear track down her cheek. "I love you, Xanthe, truly!" he said, and that precious time holding each other without moving was their 'nobody will tear us apart' moment.

She wiped her cheek and was now giggling. "Muliebrity! That's the word you need. It comes from the Latin *mulier* which means 'woman.' The word has the same derivation as *mollis* which means 'soft.' It's where the English verb 'to mollify' comes from. Sadly agápi mou, muliebrity is only used in the literary sense these days, but isn't it just wonderful? Some words make life worth living, don't you think?"

Yes, they did. For them both.

On Saturday morning at 6 am, Gideon leant on the rail of the veranda. He could hear Xanthe moving about. What were folk doing? There were fishermen and lots of shepherds. Old ladies were sweeping steps and he could see Mr Zammit, the keeper of the Citroen, driving a 1940 Australian copy of the Bedford coupé utility van to who knew where. Surely it was the prettiest open-backed utility vehicle ever built?

"What does Mr Zammit do with his time, Ma'am?" he asked.

"George? Everything," she said with pride. "Mechanic, baker, shepherd, and magistrate – he has even been known to deliver babies! Has he primed the Seven yet, agápi mou?"

"I'm not sure? I'll go and check." He went out to the back yard to find that her Citroen was washed, fuelled and most certainly ready to go.

This morning, along with an oversized white blouse, she was sporting cuffed blue jean shorts. And of course, she was discalced.

They loaded up the Citroen as the forces radio station on her tiny transistor radio tinkled out a new tune. Xanthe went to put her tea down on a precarious wooden table and started to dance like a zombie in slow motion to the opening riff of that catchy pop tune.

"You love this music don't you, Mr Trendy?" she said, as if she was really letting the repeated riff enter her soul.

"Are you stealing my music then, Miss Opera?"

"Your music, Pretty Boy?" she said as she continued to dance like a hippy. She shimmied up to him, put her arms around his neck and began to gently bite his shoulder, then kissed him all the way up his neck.

Lesson learned – music is everybody's. They set off and she drove south and stopped in the small town of Xaghra. Xanthe explained that the earliest inhabited part of Gozo was here. They looked at the Ggantija megalithic temples, which dated back to the year 3600 BC, and visited the Xaghra Stone Circle. Historically, she said, there was so much to see on this island, but there was no better place than there.

There were no tourists to be seen, except an American couple from Iowa who complained about the lack of facilities and no bathroom. Who would want a bath at this time of day, Gideon thought?

After an hour or so, they drove east to view a cave of great importance: Calypso's Cave, overlooking the glorious red sands of Ramla Beach. Xanthe said this was the cave referred to by Homer in *The Odyssey*. Homer called the island *Ogygia* and the cave was the one where the beautiful nymph Calypso kept Odysseus as a 'prisoner of love' for seven years. Gideon soaked it all in.

After an hour, they drove a mile or two south east until they came to a track at the top of a hill overlooking a bay. She took out her rucksack, smiled and crooked her finger and they started to descend a rocky goat track down to a small beach.

"You've left the keys in that incredible motor, Ma'am," he said. "Is that wise?"

"It's a good thought, Boy, but who's going to steal it? And if someone did, where are they going? They would have George to face afterwards, not only from the legal point of view but importantly, the concatenation for the thief's family would be catastrophic in this community!"

He thought he would quite like to live in a world like this, with her. Was England really that civilised?

They came to the small beach and the sand was red again. He had never even imagined red sand and now he had seen it twice in one day. They were the only people there on that small stretch of it. Xanthe unpacked, passed Gideon a beer and started changing her outfit. She put on a patterned white Lakota Sioux headband, which had a single strand of beads with a long grey and white feather hanging over her left ear and a small white feather earring in her right ear.

Her mood was casual as if she were trying to look innocent and he immediately knew that she knew precisely what she was doing as he stood there transfixed. Again!

Gideon asked her about the meaning of her aura. "I understand the word but yours seems to go beyond that to something I can't fathom."

"Beautiful you," she said. "It's something distinctive like an atmosphere or quality that seems to surround something, or someone. Some believe in a white aura, which is the hardest to see, and the rarest. You can see it in me and it means the highest stratum of spirituality and pureness. It can be associated with healing. Some would say that negative energy can be repelled by my presence alone." She curtseyed, and bowed her head and blew him a knowing kiss.

"I really do love you… *Ma'am!*" he said, exaggerating her title. She was putting her hair into two bunches with bands of beads. She then reached into her make-up bag, dipped her finger into a jar and streaked two two-inch lines across each cheek, one red and one white. This whole 'Red Indian' thing had a special effect Gideon. He shook his head in awe at the trouble she had taken to get into this character.

She took off her white blouse and blue jean shorts and she had no underwear on underneath. She simply smouldered in front of him in the midday heat. She put on a bra made to look like deerskin with tassels all around and then secured a wraparound deerskin style mini-skirt.

Getting an orange in his Christmas stocking had been an insurmountable pleasure for Gideon in the 1950s, but that gift went over the hill with its arse on fire now, as he was about to learn the true meaning of two bodies in one soul.

Her body shimmered like a mirage in the heat rising off the sand as she stood, one leg slightly bent and one hand on her curvaceous hip. She then walked towards him and said, "Hoka-Hey!"

Chapter Nineteen

The Sirocco

After an hour of dozing, holding and loving, she cracked open the wine from the insulated medical bag in her rucksack and it was just about cold enough to taste delicious. The hum of a marine engine could be heard in the distance and they watched as a boat sped around the headland, then powered off to level the hull and came slowly to a stop some one hundred yards off the beach. An anchor was slipped and when the craft had settled, the coxswain dived into the water and swam towards them on the beach.

This mariner walked up to Xanthe, accepted a glass of warm Maltese Marsovin from her, downed it in one and said, *"Stin ygeiá sas,"* then walked up the hill towards their vehicle.

"I guess Mr Zammit said cheers then, did he? How can he drink that stuff?" Gideon said, screwing up his nose.

"He most certainly did agápi mou! I see you have exquisite taste for wine now! We will swim out later and stay on the boat for the night and then steam back to the villa for Sunday."

And that's what they did. Sunbathing on the boat, lovemaking and then a light supper with copious amounts of French wine had them collapsed in the early evening in the most perfect setting ever.

The next morning Gideon woke to find his female skipper fishing naked off the stern apart from that rakish Panama hat. There were three sizeable red mullet on the deck and she gestured silently that he should gut, top and tail them, which luckily he was able to do with panache. Xanthe then rolled them in oats and flour and fried them in butter. Breakfast was unbelievably delicious.

"What would you like to do this morning, young Sir?"

she asked.

"Talk to you. Truly, I want to know who, why, how and stuff! Your language, I want to, um…"

"Be in command, take control agóri? And talk about your burgeoning oenophilia? Your growing love of all things appertaining to wine?"

"Yes, yes, all that, Ma'am!"

"Come on then, lets steam back to the villa and we will drink wine and talk!"

So they powered on through the impossibly deep blue sea towards their harbour, like movie stars on the French Riviera but without the gawping crowds. They were silent as they crossed Ramla Bay and saw nobody on that beach. It took an hour back to Marsalforn Bay and as they approached their destination, Xanthe cut the engine sharply and they drifted silently in the tiny cove just around the headland to Marsalforn. Gideon put his beer down and stood up.

She held his face with both hands and her thumbs stroked back from the corners of his eyes as she kissed him gently on his lips. He leaned forwards to kiss her, but she moved her head away and smiled. He leaned in again to caress those aubergine-coloured lips and she moved her head back and away.

He paused, then moved a third time and she gently moved both left or right in a masterly way like a sailboat inclined to port getting ready to tack and veer over to starboard. This was made even more frustrating as she was doing it to the rhythm of the boat, which was rolling and bobbing as they drifted closer to the shore. She gently held him off, staring with those adoring, tender-hearted eyes until he smiled too. She was teaching him to be patient and to take in exactly what was happening to him, to her, to them.

She disengaged and walked up to the bow and threw the anchor overboard. Xanthe sat in the large Captain's chair with her legs wide open then ripped her bikini bottoms off. Gideon struggled, clown-like, to get his shorts off without falling over. He somehow managed it, then rammed straight into her and fucked her like an animal, as if it was his last moment on this planet.

When he had ejaculated and calmed down, she tenderly held his hand and laid it flat on her stomach. "We must get to Knossos, lover," she said. He didn't know why and she said nothing more, so he kissed her. She whispered right into his ear, "There will never be anyone else, agápi mou!"

After they berthed in the small harbour, the rest of the day was spent tidying up, talking and learning and then they journeyed back to the ferry terminal. This time George gave them a lift in that pretty Bedford utility of his, and Gideon sat on a pile of sacks in the rear, occasionally holding Xanthe's manicured hand, which reached through the passenger window and rested on the roof.

They stopped for a herd of goats and an old woman with a bundle of sticks on her bent back turned to curse them, but immediately bowed her head in an apologetic gesture when she recognised Mr Zammit.

"Look!" Xanthe said with a hushed excitement at a road juncture. "It's *Monticola solitarius*!" Gideon looked amazed and confused. "It's Latin for the blue rock thrush. Didn't you do Latin in school?" she teased.

"Yes of course we did. Brass rubbings… you know, in churches." He looked at her baffled face. "What?" she had said. "The alloy is called latten and it's like brass and it's hammered out to thin strips and use for churchy stuff!"

"Churchy stuff?" she squealed with delight. "Latten? Oh! My God! How enchantingly scrumptious!"

"Shit!" he said, slapping his forehead. "You meant Latin!"

She didn't stop giggling all the way to the ferry. He felt foolish but happy. Her eyes of pure joy bored into his as she tried, unsuccessfully, to repress her bursts of laughter.

The ferry ride back to the mainland was peaceful and stunning in a 1930s traveller sort of way. He never wanted anything to change. On the ferry she only spoke once. It required no answer. "The never-ending joy of having your soul-mate love you as much as you love them is all I ever need, and that's us, Gideon."

Just before they berthed, they were letting the wind blow through their hair on the forecastle. Gideon says, "There's probably a name for this particular wind, isn't there? Oh! I bet there is!"

"Of course there is. The Navy monitors them all the time and in the sailing club, there is a constant update on these rascals that change so quickly."

"Come on then," he said. "Please?"

"God, we are going to make it, you and I, Gideon. Well, the winds are complex over Malta because it's an exposed group of islands and Sardinia and Italy both have an effect on the direction and strength of them. There is the frequent, cool *Majjistral* wind which simply means northwestern." Gideon was impressed. He was a professional seaman, why didn't he know all this?

"Also, from the northeast and well known as Malta's most feared wind, there is the *Grigal*. This is derived from the Maltese word for Greek: *Grieg*, and means 'the Greek Wind.' I know, silly, but there it is. However, this is that southerly, hair-dryer-like Sirocco breeze from Africa where my soul wants to lay forever, with you."

Her blouse was white. She was almost always in white. She was always unbearably lovely in white.

"Aeolian means with a moaning or sighing sound, or it can be a musical tone produced by the wind! Aeolus, as I mentioned, is the Greek keeper of the winds. I want to talk to you about this soon, pretty one. He is my favourite as he will send you messages. Trust me."

Gideon believed her. He wanted to know everything about this god.

Chapter Twenty

Anteros

Malta was only seventeen miles long and nine miles wide, so they found themselves back in Valletta soon enough and Xanthe booked them into the beautiful old hotel, the recently refurbished Phoenicia in Valletta town.

She had cocktails sent to their room and they showered together without making love.

As they dressed for dinner early that evening, she came towards him with a clean pair of her panties in her hand and asked Gideon to put them on. Like a rabbit caught in the headlights, he couldn't move.

She said softly, "This is not a game, young man, it's so you will never forget me!"

He slipped them on and finished dressing, and far from feeling awkward, he felt full-blooded, as of course she knew he would. Indeed, he had never felt as masculine as he melted into her being.

"Let's hope this doesn't lead to cryptovestiphilia!" she teased. He didn't know what that meant, but hoped it was rude.

Dinner was around the corner in a cosy Maltese bistro. There he was captivated by Xanthe's story of Odysseus and his twenty-year journey home from the Trojan War. He had terrific adventures along the way, and many changes of fortune, she said. It was also a voyage of discovery of his psychological and spiritual feelings. So Gideon was having his first odyssey, then – a short one but no less powerful for that.

"Give me a sentence that describes you best?" she said suddenly, putting her fork down, elbows on the table and clenched hands under her chin.

He chuckled, "My mother would disapprove of your elbows being on the table. Imagine, Ma looking down on *you*?! So, a sentence about me… Fair, understanding and loyal. Unusual for my age, I think. I've fucked up many times, but I've always been loyal! Excuse my French, Ma'am."

"Very understandable, young Sir. I love the way the English use that expression when they excuse themselves for their profanities! Did you know that the Arabic nations are famous for their cursing? The Gauls can be beastly too, but in Arabic, well, it's perfectly normal, so it doesn't offend anyone."

"But I like offending the French, Ma'am!" he said with a genuine frown.

"Of course you do, it is an English sport, but if you want to insult, degrade or just plain upset the French, remind them of their history. Admire their culture, their cinema, their food and their vision, but don't mention their politics and most definitely not their history. They hate that."

"Excuse my Arabic, then," he said.

She picked up her wine glass full of Bordeaux, chinked his glass, raised hers and said; "Fuck that French, then, eh, *mon amour?*"

As they we walked back to the hotel arm in arm, Xanthe was in a quieter mood. "Your biggest enemy will be ignorance," she whispered in a doleful tone. "It appears in many forms. The problem starts with people's misinterpretation of the word." He clearly didn't understand so she continued in a more uplifting manner. "There's 'object ignorance,' which is just an unacquaintance with a particular object and that can be understandable and not necessarily a bad thing. Then there is 'technical ignorance,' which is lacking the basic knowledge of how to do something. Then there is my *bête noire*, 'factual ignorance.'"

He liked this train of thought.

"This is understandable in some cases. If one doesn't know certain facts, then so be it, but some facts should be known. I mean, what's the capital of England? Well, if someone didn't know that…! What language do they speak in the 'country' of Europe, or is sixty seconds the same as one minute? You know, that level of ignorance."

"Surely that's just stupidity?"

"Oh! No, agápi mou. A vast difference between the two words. Wait until you get to America. The best of the best and the worst of the worse!" She smiled knowingly.

Truly, she was wisdom itself!

And with that, they were at the foyer of the hotel. Although recently updated, it still had an old Mediterranean charm. The bar was full of scientists and backers of the archaeological digs in Gozo. Due to her passion for history, her connections and language skills, Xanthe was part of this crowd. Some of them, although not the archaeology team, looked at her and then at him, first in awe (lucky him!) then curiosity (how could she?). What impressed him was her absolute belief in the two of them. She showed such a lack of concern, so who knew how she felt? His quiet confidence grew.

Xanthe gently steered Gideon towards a group of men who she said he should meet as they had the means to take her all over the world and that of course, meant him, too.

At the edge of that crowd, Gideon spotted Mr Hinkley with two other officers from St Angelo. Hinkley looked surprised but recovered quickly when he saw them and Gideon thought his eyes showed a sadness within.

Far from being phased when he told her, Xanthe raised her eyebrows in mocking pleasure and walked over to speak to him. "Good evening, Nigel, how delightful to see a Pecksniffian!"

Mr Hinkley seemed to be trying to find appropriate words to reply, but just spluttered, "Xanth! *Hi!*"

Gideon had no idea what 'Pecksniffian' meant, but he knew it was negative and that she had said 'delightful' to hide its true meaning. How delicious, he thought, her rapier wit demolishing that awful man.

"Please call me Ma'am. If you must call me Xanthe when we're in mufti, there is an E on the end and it would be more respectful for you to get it right."

Gideon's face remained neutral and he held eye contact with Mr Hinkley. The officer would know that he had a weekend pass to visit the sites with these experts, so the two of them being there would normally be no cause for concern.

Xanthe was being discrete and cautious and yet he could see her thinking they might be on to her, but right then, she was enjoying the mystery and guessing games.

"How did you find the digs?" Mr Hinkley asked Gideon. The question was a test of course and he noted that Hinkley did not use his name or rank.

"Overawed, Sir!" Gideon beamed. "I learnt from First Officer Craven that Calypso's Cave is thought to be the one from Homer's *Odyssey*, Sir." To add to his daring, he was erotically aware of the lacy underwear that encased his manliness and the feeling now gave him new vigour. "Homer says that the Gozitan sea nymph, Calypso, had Odysseus enslaved here for seven years until he legged it, I mean… escaped, Sir, and returned to his wife. Ma'am says that Homer wrote *The Odyssey* somewhere between 750–650 BC, nearly 3,000 years ago. The very fact that you can visit a cave that was featured in a book from that period blows my mind. I hope that when the British leave, the new Government will look after it, Sir?"

"Isn't he just wonderful, *Nige*?" Xanthe said.

The frustrated, angry, maybe even jealous officer said; "Quite so!" and stormed off to the bar.

Nobody could hear them as the noise rose in the bustling hotel bar. Still, Xanthe put a flat palm on the lapel of Gideon's jacket, leaned slightly towards his ear and breathed, "I love you, baby."

Xanthe went to seek out the manager to order champagne and something to eat for the room. Gideon thought how wonderful and out of whack that she had rented the room for the night and ordered bubbly in Catholic-oppressed Malta! If you walked these narrow streets on a Sunday morning, knowing how fervent the followers of religion were, you would not believe what went on behind some closed doors. He did not agree with the religious types, but admired their loyalty.

The manager bowed as they climbed the stairs to the suite, and he was either a beautiful man who was helping love blossom on this island, or a pervert who had a secret spyhole onto their double bed, Gideon thought.

In the room he turned to face her and she put her hands gently on his shoulders. He leaned forward quickly to caress those aubergine lips with his, and she moved her head back and away slightly. He then moved in a second time and she moved to avoid him, precisely as she had done that morning at sea. Far from waiting until he started to look perplexed or angry, she would gently hold him off, staring at him with tender-hearted eyes until he breathed out and looked at her lovingly. Only then would she let him advance and take what was his after all that pea cocking. His desire was so strong and her control was so intoxicating.

"How do you know that we're not being watched through a spyhole Ma'am?" Gideon said, undressing.

"What would you think if that were true?"

"Well, voyeurism is something the boys on board like. Weeks ago I wouldn't have minded, but this is too precious to share, Ma'am."

"My God, how wonderful of you!" she said. "Let's discretely look then, shall we?"

They looked at the only real places there could be a peep-hole facing the bed and there were none. Xanthe slipped out her dress and sat on the edge of the bed, saying, "I'm a little disappointed!" Gideon was about to announce his horror when he realised she was joking.

She held both arms out. He took her hands and sat with her. With one leg beneath her, she let out a thoughtful sigh. "Don't ever think this is ephemeral, Gideon. Way back in the depths of time, dreamers and lovers conceived a flower that never died. They called it 'Amaranth' to represent eternal love. The word is from my language and has its root in 'Amarantos' which means unfading – immortal if you like. You can say 'amaranthine' to refer to an imaginary flower and anything with its undying quality! I'm not like the melancholic Cio-Cio San, Miss Butterfly's name in Japanese; I don't believe this is unrequited?"

"I don't understand all of what you say, but I can feel it, Ma'am, truly!"

"I know you can. I adore the way you use the word 'truly.' It's your way of saying 'listen to me, I am being honest.' And stop calling me Ma'am, you delicious thing!"

She kissed him and whispered, "One fine day I will see a wisp of smoke rising over the farthest edge of the sea." He didn't know where that was from, but he loved the silence after she said it.

After making love, she fell asleep in his arms but not before she said, so quietly that he had to lean closer to hear, "I love so you so deeply, Gideon. Ataraxia for me at last."

She meant that serene calm she had told him about. He stayed awake with wine in hand as long as he could just to watch her in her circadian rhythms. He took his watch off for the first time he could remember since he was a boy so as not to know the time. He wanted it to stand still.

Gideon knew by then that Cupid is a Roman translation of Eros and usually associated with love of all kinds, but Cupid in Roman mythology is strictly sexual lust! Xanthe had told him this, and that Eros meant true love. She had also told him about Anteros, the god of requited love. Gideon lay there convinced that Anteros was in their room that evening.

Chapter Twenty-One

A changed man

As Gideon dressed the next morning, he said, "If I never saw you again, I would be complete."

"Me also. Now go back, and I will sort this out. I know you are not the type to gloat, and don't be tempted. Men of Mr Hinckley's ilk enjoy their power. I know you will be strong. Dignity at all costs, lover."

As Gideon walked away, she tucked her finger into his waistband and said, "You mention that you have the rank of Ordinary Seaman? How very unbeautiful and absurd. You are not ordinary, agápi mou, and I don't think you ever will be."

It made him believe that he was someone. Not exceptional, but just someone to somebody which indeed, he now was.

"May I quote Nietzsche?" she said suddenly. "He said; 'The higher we soar, the smaller we appear to those who cannot fly.'"

He kissed her. He got it. "You can quote whoever you want to me... Xanthe."

Gideon walked up the gangway to the flight deck and the kindly Quartermaster, known as 'Jazz,' handed him his station card. Mr Hinkley was on the flight deck too and Gideon averted his eyes but had to squeeze past the man to get down into the mortar well and then on to the mess deck.

Gideon knew he smelled of patchouli oil, Xanthe's preferred fragrance, and he knew that the jealous one would know where he had been. "Excuse me, Sir," he said to the silly little man, who was not letting him pass.

Gideon engaged eye contact with the officer and for the first time in his life thought of rebelling, saying something sarcastic or even slightly rude – but Xanthe was right next to him in this head and it gave him more power than the other man, with his little game. What had Xanthe said, 'prurient parlour games'? He smiled and said again, "Sir?"

The man stepped aside. Gideon held onto both rails and without his feet touching the steps, slid down the ladder with an assuredness that he had never had before. Mickey had told him not to do this. "If there's bit of grease on that rail or it's wet, you'll break your neck!" he had warned.

"But you do it all the time, Mick!"

"Do as I say matey, not as I fucking do!" But this time, Gideon got away with it.

The day was filled with the regular business of keeping a vessel shipshape. A fuel barge was due and another Ordinary Seaman, Smudge Smith, and Gideon were standing on the Port waist laughing at some of the insane things that were happening at that time. Just then, Mr Hinkley came out of the Wardroom flat door and walked towards them. One would not necessarily stand to attention when an officer walked by on board, but maybe as a mark of respect, straighten up and say, 'Good morning, Sir' or the like. But they weren't going to do that for this small and arrogant man.

Mr Hinkley snapped, "Haven't you any work to do, because if not, I have a mind to put you both on a charge of idling with intent!"

Smudge said, "With intent to do what Sir? You are surely having a laugh, aren't you?"

Before Hinkley could reply, Gideon said casually, "Well, there's a fuel barge steaming toward us and we are the berthing party for the approaching vessel, Sir."

Mr Hinkley seemed shocked that anyone could be so laid-back whilst talking to him.

"You know, Sir, we have to tie the bits of string that they will throw up to us so it will be secure alongside us. So we can take on fuel, Sir, but if you like, we could go and ask Leading Seaman King if there are any decks that need to be scrubbed. I'm sure the Officer of the Day will gladly take the front bit of the stringy thing and maybe you could take the back bit. Sir?"

He was being out of order, but his patience at the officer's attitude was wearing thin.

Smudge turned to Gideon. "Fuel barges don't steam, matey. It has to be secured to a tug like this one is coming towards us, don't it?"

"Smudge!"

"Yes?"

"Shut the ever-loving fuck up!"

How they laughed. It was hard to tell whether it was Gideon's insolence or the laughter that prompted Mr Hinkley to put Gideon on a charge for insubordination.

Gideon went below decks to get his cap and reported to the Regulating Office, the naval equivalent to a police station. The kind and gentle Master-at-Arms tutted and asked what had he done and he explained what had happened, leaving out his sarcasm, of course.

The Master-at-Arms stood up and Gideon observed that he did not button up his jacket. The Master sighed heavily, "Right, off you go, lad, I'll sort this out."

And indeed, he did, much to everyone's relief. Smudge denied everything he had heard and all was well, but the concatenation would not stop there.

Gideon had learned that on a professional warship, everyone had to work together. No matter how happy a ship is, there are always people who are different to the Navy's conceived ethos and who swim against the tide. They were usually easily dealt with, but the problem here, everyone knew, was the temperament of this young, inexperienced officer who was meant to become a leader of men. He had disruptive power that he thought would rough-ride a thousand years of history.

"Some toffs don't like oiks, Gids. Don't take it to heart. You just have to beat them," said Mickey. "Fucking pickle jar officers!" He went on without Gideon saying a word, "Pickle jar officers are well educated, and you know, university toffs and all that. They'll know the square root of the lid of that jar within two bleedin' jiffies, but can't get the fucking thing off!"

Gideon spat his tea out laughing, not because it was funny, but because Mickey was quite serious.

"The thing is, Nipper, when they can't do something or get shown up in front of folk, all they can think of is destroy, destroy, destroy!"

Mickey's first thoughts were now damage limitation. "We have to be vulpine, my friend," he said with his hand on Gideon's shoulder, shaking him gently to show that he was going to be alright.

Gideon felt quite overcome with emotion, but knew that Mickey would require a nautical reaction. "What the fuck does 'vulpine' mean Mick?"

It sounded as though they were in a game now, and one that Mickey thought they could win. The problem for Gideon was that this was no game as love filled his heart with every beat. And they didn't realise that things were about to escalate.

Secure was piped at midday and after a steaming hot shower, Mickey and Gideon stepped ashore. A scruffy but charming pub in the old city was fun but Gideon's mind was in a different place.

He was having the most insane conversation with Mickey and strangely, he learned new words from him too. Vulpine being one earlier, but his favourite today was, *Déjà brew*. He laughed at how different people used the English language, and missed his Greek lover.

At the bar, Mickey was ribbing a pretty lady, trying to impress her and her friends. They were the nurses from the hospital at Kalkara.

Gideon walked over to talk to the one who had touched his arm the other day. "You look lovely," he said. "I really like screen-printed dresses and the colour of the flowers on yours matches your eyes."

She seemed pleased at the observation. "My name is Viveka, but everyone calls me Viv. Buy me a drink and come sit with me," she said and touched his arm again. Gideon was flattered and confident, as his heart was already taken.

Suddenly, and loudly, he heard another nurse snap at

Mickey. "How is it that you blokes can shag many women and suddenly, you're a fucking legend, but if a girl does two guys in a year, she's a slut?"

"Fuckin' easy," says Mick the oracle. The room went quiet, just like in the movies. "Confucius once said that if a key opens a lot of locks, it's a master key. But if lots of keys open a single lock, it's a shitty fucking lock!"

There was rapturous applause and much back-slapping, as if the guys were mimicking gorillas. It was a funny story, but Gideon saw the sadness and sheer loneliness of the nurse on the end of the put-down. She was distraught. He had a deep desire to walk across that room and comfort her. He couldn't, though, not in front of everyone. He loathed his cowardice. And then in a flash, he put his glass down and started to walk towards her, when Mickey grabbed his arm.

Mickey pulled him aside in all that chaos and said seriously, "When have you ever heard a woman tell a good story, my friend?" Gideon didn't understand and wanted to tell Mickey about Xanthe and her wondrous stories. But then he realised that this was a lesson he was being taught about the man's world in which he served. And so he bottled out.

Later he vowed that he would never stand by again and watch someone get hurt.

Chapter Twenty-Two

Interrogation

The mood had been ruined in the bar. Some were still laughing and some were angry. Mickey said, "You stay with what you pulled, matey, we're off to the Gut!"

Gideon was swimming against Mickey's flow for the first time. On one hand, the story was funny, but the hurt that it had caused left him ashamed. All the nurses had left the bar except Viveka. Gideon bought her another drink and they talked of the sad situation.

"I saw what you were going to do, but blokes will be blokes!" Viveka said with a shrug.

"I know," said Gideon, "but if you saw a guy kicking a puppy, who wouldn't walk across the road to intervene?" He hated his actions. After a pleasant hour with her, they parted good friends and he thought of Jyoti as he watched her walk away into the crowds.

Sometimes it seemed that the heat never relented, even as winter approached. Gideon loved the warmth and yet thought of autumnal days in England. He loved the buzz of history in the making as an outpost of the UK was closed down, like dismantling the set of a play. White-painted stones around flag poles were being moved, pictures of the Queen taken off walls, regimental plaques taken down and everything English was being packed into crates. The balmy air heightened the feel of it for Gideon.

In one apartment the Navy had acquired for married personnel on the island, the name of the Dorset village *Piddletrenthide* was being left behind on the door of a now empty room. This had made a two-minute news story back in England, and that's how Gideon saw this great upheaval of lives. It was just a glitch. Never mind, pull those shoulders back, and carry on! It was sad in a way for the service personnel who had loved the place, but overall life was moving on.

Taking Mickey's advice, Gideon was mentally photographing it all and taking notes in case he ever needed to regale someone with the tale. His main impression was that the English were happy to be going home and the Maltese were worried about their economy without the English pound. Mass tourism was going to be their only lifeline. Excitement was the buzzword, however. Whichever side of the situation you were on, it was exciting!

On board there were too many questions about Gideon. Where was he going? Why did he look so happy about it? Why didn't he want to get drunk and go whoring? So much so, that he was called into his Divisional Officer's cabin. Gideon had no respect for this amphibian-looking, badly dressed man. He seemed to him to be a grown-up version of Mr Hinkley. He asked many questions about Gideon's whereabouts and actions but appeared ambivalent about having to do so. Gideon could either answer them or fob him off with a specious explanation. Then he was told to report to join a different work detail in the morning and report to an Army officer at some barracks that he had never heard of. It sounded ominous.

In the morning, several of the crew drove up to St Andrew's Barracks, just north of the capital, where a Royal Marine Commando Unit was based. The work detail joined a group of soldiers but Gideon was led to a dusty old tin-roofed hut, which seemed crazy in this heat. He walked through the door, where there was an Army Sergeant sitting at a desk with a small oblong sign in red, which read, 'Intelligence Unit.'

The Sergeant told Gideon to go through to the office behind him. There were two officers: a Royal Marine standing and an Army Major, sitting. Good cop, bad cop, was Gideon's first thought and he was beginning to get worried.

Good cop (Army) asked Gideon about the weekend away on the dig and he answered truthfully that it was amazing. He had enough knowledge to display about what he had learned of Calypso's Cave and the history of the Phoenician period and he was proud of his composure and ability to hold his own with these people.

Initially, their main concern was that he might have been dating a local girl and they were very concerned about the 'British Passport thing,' also known as the 'golden chalice' that many ladies sought. He didn't mind the informal chat, but he was genuinely scared of the outcome.

It was Gideon who got the ball rolling, saying, "Is there a problem, Sir?" with casual arrogance.

Now the bad cop (Royal Marine) interjected, "What do you think of First Officer Craven... *Seaman*?"

Seaman? How unnecessary! Gideon knew that the pause and the emphasis on the word was meant to be offensive as in 'semen,' like he was some sort of stain. But then Gideon smiled, thinking this was one of Xanthe's homophones. Spelled differently and yet pronounced the same.

"Very pretty, Sir. Hard to keep my thoughts on the dig sometimes and I suppose it's just a male thing. I mean we are not compatible on any level and never will be as long as my arse points downward Sir, pardon my Arabic, but she is very kind to me and I love the way she speaks and..."

Bad cop put his hand up, palm towards Gideon. "Sub-Lieutenant Hinkley has reported to his superior that you were drinking with her at the Phoenicia Hotel on Monday evening?"

"Yes Sir, I was." The speed of his admission surprised them. "She had also taken me to dinner before the party and explained all about Homer's *Odyssey* Sir. I love history and I was never taught like that at school, so I'm just eager to learn. That's what interests me for sure, Sir." The bad cop backed down.

After about thirty minutes, and many pointless questions, the rotten cop left and the good cop offered Gideon a cigarette. He shook his head. The kind Army Officer spoke in a gentle and kindly tone. "We are not blind, young man and we are not stupid."

He rambled on, saying that he thought he knew what was happening with Gideon and that he couldn't spare the manpower to watch him all the time to find out where he went, so he asked him to come clean.

"It's like I say, Sir, First Officer Craven is just ebullient and full of passion about everything. She even speaks a different language to most and I'm absolutely soaking it all in because I know this will be ephemeral…"

"Yes. One begins to speak like her now doesn't one?"

One most certainly does, thought Gideon and tried not to smile.

"Right. Carry on, Sailor and I'll be in touch if I hear any more about this unusual situation."

On the transport back to Valletta he was thinking that they might both be discharged and they would live happily ever after in rural England and Pooh-sticks to the Navy. Or somewhere in Greece, maybe?

The next morning Gideon was engrossed in myriad thoughts and in the sights and sounds of the dismantling of the Empire. He was cheerful as he turned up at a dusty village, where a service wife was dressed as a local even though her husband was a Sergeant in the Signal Corps. They were both English but had gone native!

He was alive with the anticipation of meeting Xanthe. Every thought, every moment of every day was filled with this captivating woman.

Chapter Twenty-Three

The Oedipus complex

Gideon could not drag Mickey along every time he needed to be at a covert meeting and so he had to go along with some other shipmates on occasions and would let them move on as he browsed through long-playing discs in a record shop. Bizarrely to Gideon, Valletta had an up to date selection of music deep in the middle of these chaotic city streets. He then bought a disc, jumped in a taxi and headed north to Sliema.

Gideon walked into a hotel bar and picked out Xanthe, looking graceful sitting sipping her wine. He stopped just to look at her and admire her from a distance. She turned her head and immediately stood up as he approached and hugged her tightly.

Xanthe gently pulled him down next to her. "You really do alter your whole being when you are touched or hugged," she said and asked if this was really a new sensation to him? He told her that he had never been held before as though he was the only person who mattered in the world. The only time he could remember being held was when he was having his hair dried by his mother. He would have been five or six years old and he loved being close to her breasts, albeit in an asexual way. She said that Sigmund Freud had written about this complex in his *Interpretation of Dreams*.

"I knew that!" Gideon joked, "I was only yesterday reading the same essay." He wafted his wrist at her as if to say 'Run along with you, fair maiden' and she laughed and shook her head and those dark eyes bored into his soul.

"It is called the Oedipus complex in Freud's psychoanalytic theory. A desire for sexual involvement with the parent of the opposite sex and sometimes there is a sense of rivalry with the father."

Gideon didn't understand and certainly did not have any

thought of sleeping with his mother.

"Crucially," she said, catching his expression, "it is normal in a boy's development process."

"Really?" he said, calming down slightly.

"Yes, if you were brought up harmoniously, then the stage passes."

"Where does the name come from?" Gideon asked, liking these bits best.

"From our myth of the boy Oedipus, who kills his father and unwittingly marries his mother. There are dreadful acts of self-mutilation when he finds out what he has done. But the Oedipus complex, or 'conflict' in my opinion, arises simply because the boy develops a libido and therefore sexual yearnings for his mother. He wants to possess his mother solely for himself and get rid of his father to enable him to do so. It is normal and it is common."

Gideon's head was spinning.

"It passes in a harmonious household." She then looked at him and he thought she was going to cry and yet she just whispered; "I love you so very deeply, boy."

The next morning when Gideon was talking about Oedipus in the quarter deck locker, Mickey said: "So it's alright to fuck your mother is it, Gids?" And he collapsed with laughter. "Fuckin' well is in Alabama, my friend!" he said with a knowing glint in his eye. We think we're the benchmark of how society should be, don't we? I mean, justice, love and marriage, Christian God and all!"

"That's a bit deep for you, isn't it, Mickey?"

"Yes, but as you travel around the world, you see stuff that just don't make sense to you. The thing is, you have to try and understand what other people are thinking and that's what makes us different."

"What do you mean?"

"Well, I've seen sister shagging in some religious sect in upstate New York and that's supposed to be the most sophisticated society in the world, innit? But the point is that it was totally acceptable to them! I ain't saying its right, I'm saying, to them it's OK! I've seen an Arab fuck his goats

113

and I've seen a son in the Balkans think it's perfectly normal to shag his mum. You said you had tingles when your mother dried your hair, but you didn't want to fuck her, did you? I'm saying that it certain situations, well, they would do that stuff. Very common in many parts of the globe, Giddy. Christ, I need a beer."

So did Gideon.

"Another thing, matey, I knew a matelot from Watford who loved his mother so much, well, they was a thing, you know... Taboo love ain't always wrong, Gids, I'm just saying..." He tailed off into a confused silence.

"What's the answer, Mick?"

"Beer, me old sunshine, plenty of fucking beer, so get those wets in, toot-sweet!"

As they clicked their tins of ale, Mickey shook his head and says; "*Furiosior Undis*" and before he could ask what it meant, Mickey just carried on with, "It was the Motto of HMS Cassandra, a ship I served on some years ago, and it translates to 'madder than the waves' and in the Navy, it means beyond the pale or hard to fuckin' fathom! That Latin, they have a word for the part of your mind that is entirely unconscious but has hidden desires and needs, and it's called the 'id.' For fuck's sake! What kinda word is a fucking id?" He laughed so heartily that Gideon thought he would burst.

"How do you know that, Mickey?"

"Because it's a Scrabble word. Some clown always challenges my words so I have to know my onions, don't I?"

They raised their beer cans and both said "fuck it" in unison. The Oedipus complex really was healthy and normal then, and they decided to the whole 'id' thing could be sorted out another day.

Chapter Twenty-Four

T L Sea

Christmas Eve was on a Friday and Gideon did not have to be back on board until 0730 on the Monday morning, having secured another weekend pass. It was warm and he had lost any inhibitions he might have had at the beginning of the affair. Secrecy was essential of course, but the city was chaotic and he was beginning to enjoy the ruse. Not in a cocky way, but confident. He took the *dghajsa* across the harbour and then the Barrakka Lift up to the Gardens. He then walked northeast across the city, occasionally looking over his shoulder, wondering if he would catch a glimpse of a gumshoe with his trilby pulled over one eye.

No such person was following him, so he jumped into a taxi, which took him to Sliema. He was feeling pleasantly refreshed and entered a wonderfully run-down and basic bar. If it had been empty, one would probably not have guessed it was a bar except for the small, rickety tables, each with a checkerboard on and of course, the ubiquitous ashtrays. It was full of Maltese folk and one dashing beauty in a white dress with a Panama hat covering her eyes, who was easy to spot in the sepia scene.

He made his way through the bustling place to the foreigner in white. "I am from another time, Ma'am, and I have come to take you back to Gozo to stop time."

"Why, handsome God," she said. "I'll come with you with pleasure, for I am a prisoner of your heart now and you can do what you will with me and one hopes that the time stopping will be eternal. But first, a cold beer?"

"Too bloody right, Ma'am, I mean, yes please, most definitely!"

"Right, two bloody beers it is then!" She waved to a lady. The lady brought the beers to the table in two clean chipped glasses and Gideon wouldn't want it any other way now.

The two women talked in Maltese and yet Gideon grasped the meaning of what was being said through their tones. Pleasing, loving, hopeful and perfect for this setting.

After a pleasant pair of hours drinking and talking, they slowly walked along the road through Gzira with the harbour on their left, arms around each other, towards Manoel Island. The island was attached to Gzira by a roadway, with the old fort dominating the small, perfect, leaf-shaped piece of land.

Fort Manoel had a rich history and was worth visiting at any time, but he was wondering with a smile why they were heading for it now. He said nothing as this lady did nothing without good reason. If they had walked there, turned around and walked back, then that would have been just fine, as it was magical on every level.

They walked across the bridge towards the fortress and then down to the yacht marina.

"This club really is one of the last bastions of the British Empire, agápi mou," she said. "Patronised by lots of blustery old Colonel types, all talking of how the world is going to pieces and this includes the Navy of course. The club only moved here last year from Floriana and it has not built its boundaries as yet. I have good friends of my father who let me use the facilities here, which includes this!"

There, in front of them was a one hundred and thirty-eight-foot twin-masted Schooner, which she said was something like a hundred years old. It was American, sleek and beautiful. They walked some yards further along the quay and there was a much smaller motor yacht. "This one is also American and wouldn't one just know it?" she said with a smile. "It is a sixty-four foot Huckins, built in 1964, so she is reasonably new and belongs to one of my father's closest friends. He named it after his feelings for his wife."

Gideon looked at the name: 'T L Sea.'

"He is a man of probity and currently serving in the Far East, coordinating the pulling out of that area. Doing what we are doing, but over there!" she said, giggling.

They walked up the gangway, she produced a key and

they descended into a lounge area. You could tell that this was a craft for pleasure as opposed to the super yacht ahead of them, such was the opulence of the furnishings.

Xanthe went to the bar, opened a bottle of Chablis and poured two glasses. She then sat down, watching Gideon and breathed out a gasp of air. He turned to face her and he couldn't find any words to say to her as this was the first time that she did not take control straight away. Perhaps she was letting him step up to the next stratum of manhood?

The silence, save the gentle lap of water on the hull, commingled with her powerful patchouli aroma with the heady mix of grain and grape they had drunk made this moment surreal for him.

Xanthe pulled her dress up above her knees, crossed her legs and sat back in the soft furnishings. Testosterone pumped through his body and made him pulsate with anticipation. He stepped towards her and she unbuckled his shorts and pushed them to the deck. He looked down and semen was leaking from the tip of his erect penis and she pinched a globule between her thumb and forefinger and put that finger on her tongue. He wanted to explode right then and so she gently knelt, took the erect member in her mouth and allowed him the release he so desired.

She then sat on the chart table, gently put his flagging phallus inside her and as the blood drained away from the shaft, she orgasmed violently over it and then held him tightly, her fingernails breaking the skin of his back.

She stood up and took a mouthful of wine, swilled it around her mouth then engaged Gideon's lips and transferred it for him to swallow.

She went in the sleeping cabin and changed into sawn-off shorts and a big white billowing shirt, which she knotted at the front, and they held each other like silent movie stars in a Charlie Chaplin flick.

"Tell me what you think about deeply and what you believe you are good at, agápi mou?" she said later as they sat down to eat.

"Gosh? Well, I think the world is changing now because

people are appalled with our English history and our past conduct because it doesn't fit in with their modern-day sensitivities. A bit heavy, I know. I mean, I don't agree with women not being able to vote, but if I lived in 1918 after the Great War, well, who knows? Deep thoughts have made me kind of different to my school friends. As for what I'm good at, geography and football is the answer and I'm mad about history, too."

She spoke softly, "I can't believe your parents missed all this, my love. And history is essential, lest we forget!"

She paused and Gideon saw a tear appear in the corner of her eye.

"Oh! No!" he said quickly, "Don't feel sorry for me – I'm turning out to be who I wanted to be. Truly!"

She nodded. "Sport can be used in a good way to get people with little education up and into the world with pride, and the services do that too. I like very much the fact that you used to dream in the school library. You were already reaching out, were you not?"

"I guess so. I remember listening to a Beach Boys documentary on the wireless and although the music was sublime to me, it was America in the background that changed everything in me. You know, the drive-through burger bars, the big Chevys, the attitude... you know, America as opposed to tardy ol' Dorset!" She looked him with those big, dark eyes. "I wanted to find out about it in the school library, and by reading American history, I fell in love with my country's past too. Silly isn't it? The TV shows were very good if a little cheesy, but why did they speak English? How come everything seemed bigger and better over there? Oh! I don't know, but I knew I couldn't stay in Dorset any longer than I had to. George Formby's black and white, rain-soaked ukulele compared to the Beach Boys sunny and exciting Theremin music? It was easy and natural for me."

"Beautiful metaphor, beautiful you!" she said.

For the meal, they had grilled sardines and plain *Christopsomo* bread which they dipped in olive oil. Simple and delicious, it was called 'Christ bread,' she explained. It was a round loaf that is a staple of the Greek Christmas table, eaten on Christmas Eve.

"The decoration varies throughout the many different regions of my country," she said, "and the women mould the dough to represent the household's life and work. Almonds are sprinkled on top to symbolise prosperity. I am not religious, but I had the cross baked in the centre of this one as it wouldn't be right to not have it there on this special day for the Greeks. TLC methinks, young man?"

He could not think of any meal in his life that had been so simple and so lovely. Tender, loving care indeed then.

Chapter Twenty-Five

It's all Greek to me

Gideon asked Xanthe about the history of her country, and she was delighted to answer. "Our history is unlike yours, agápi mou. Although the ancient part goes so far back, we were only recognised as a modern-day nation in 1832. Quite young in comparison to England."

"Is that all?" Gideon teased.

"No that's not nearly all, you cheeky boy! That is my summary. Under the protocol signed at the London Conference that year between the protecting powers of Russia, France and good old Britain, Greece was defined as an independent country and finally shook off the Ottoman yoke."

"The Ottoman yoke?" he had said slowly. "That's a metaphor, isn't it?"

"Of course it is, funny old you. Often, I have my first sundowner during the Last Dog Watch on board here at 1832 hours, to remember Greek independence," she purred, making a drinking gesture.

Later, he watched her deep in thought on the quarterdeck, wine in hand. She turned around to face him and spoke softly but with a serious tone. "I have a charming house in a place called Nafplion, Gideon. It is a seaport town in the Peloponnese region, on the Argolic Gulf. It's a Venetian style town with Greek roots, and was our first capital, which all makes it unique and magical. It can be reached from Athens in a little over two hours..." she faded away quietly. Gideon knew what she was thinking.

He jumped in quickly. "I'm getting asked some awkward questions on board, but I hold my own, Ma'am. I think I piss them off with my confidence."

"Yes, I have been asked many questions, too," she said. She started to speak but seemed to be struggling to find the right words for the first time since they had met. He was becoming concerned, seeing his angel with her wings clipped, but then she said, "I have money and powerful associates and I have to ask you, if we were to…"

He moved swiftly to her and said, "Yes!" and her eyes became moist. Gideon knew then what the *we* meant.

The rest of the evening was quiet and loving on that motor yacht in the harbour and it was the perfect setting for their mood. There was a 'we' and that was all that mattered.

The next morning was Christmas day. After making furious love, Xanthe cried uncontrollably in Gideon's arms for nearly thirty time-stopping minutes. She then produced a silver bracelet with the Greek key design from her purse. "It's mine and I have treasured it since I saw it. It would mean just everything to me that you wear it only when you want time to stand still."

Gideon took his watch off immediately and put the charm on his wrist.

She was deadly serious when she spoke again. "Jealousy can affect some people in a dreadful way. They feel the need to match or surpass someone they envy. They usually do it by imitation, but sometimes it's worse, they use intimidation. Or even destruction."

Gideon knew who she meant. Her tone chilled him.

"Mr Hinkley has picayune, small-minded beliefs, which are abhorrent for a British officer. I think he honestly believes that other races and social classes are inferior to his and that, sadly, my love, includes you. He doesn't have any broad or open views, and his petty ones cloud his judgments and opinions."

Gideon knew that everything she said had a purpose and a meaning, and listened, fascinated. Suddenly, a bell clapped just once in a small church across the bay and she said without looking up, "Hardly a mellifluous tintinnabulation was it, agápi mou?"

He smiled in awe. "I just love the way you speak the English language."

"French is the language of love, Italian for romance and

seduction, Spanish for passion. One could swap round all those languages and purposes it would still be true. But English wouldn't fit into this group, would it?"

"What about Greek?" he asked.

She shook her head from side to side very slowly as if to tease him and said, "Have you heard of the expression 'It's all Greek to me?' Well, that pretty much says everything. Greek is a complex communication tool, and it doesn't need to fit into this seductive group, does it?"

Gideon shook his head. "You are amazing. Beyond belief. And seductive? Who knows?"

Chapter Twenty-Six

Teardrop on a wine glass

"When we first spoke," Gideon said, "you said that you were with your 'chime.' Please Miss, what's a chime?"

She smiled. "Chime is a collective noun for the bird *Troglodytes,* commonly known as the Wren…" He sipped his wine and thought excitedly, here she goes again! "I have another word for you," she said. "You need to know *sentient*, my love as it means being responsive to your sense impressions, or conscious of them anyway. A sentient person is one who perceives and responds to sensations of whatever kind, you know, smell and taste, and sight and what one hears." She pondered and then went on. "You were sentient when that pretty little nurse, and my goodness she was pretty, touched your arm. It moved me. Deeply."

"I met her again recently in a rowdy bar in the old city. I bought her a drink," Gideon said with not a suspicion that it would bother her.

He was correct. "Good for you, sweet boy."

Sleeping next to her was the closest thing to heaven he could ever perceive. The next morning, they woke up naturally at 0400 and made gentle, passionate love. Xanthe sometimes slowed him down or slid off him when he was about to come too soon, or just stopped him completely so he could catch his breath and take in what was happening. Then she would release him and match his eager excitement.

In the galley later, she handed Gideon a cold beer. It was not quite nine o'clock in the morning and they were drinking beer? As if she could read his thoughts, she suddenly said. "We've been awake for four hours, so technically, it is lunch time for us!" He agreed wholeheartedly. She was looking ritzy in her white underwear with a white, oversized blouse billowing in the breeze coming through the porthole.

"I could live like this forever, Xanthe. I mean it," he said.

"Yes, I like your train of thought. Truly I do. Was it not Epictetus who wrote 'Opulence consists not in having many possessions but in having few wants?'"

"I think it was! I remember him talking to me down in the Dog and Duck in Clapham about it, man, he can be such an arsehole sometimes..." said Gideon and they both laughed at his mimicry.

She looked out at the harbour. "So little viridity on these islands! They have been inhabited since around 5900 BC. By farmers initially and their crude methods degraded the soil so the islands became uninhabitable." Gideon's expression must have given him away: why would she bring this up now? "The only thing that is green on these islands, Mr Curious, are those green doors of yours!" she teased.

She talked about their relationship, then. She said the physical side was deep and meaningful, but it was the meeting of two souls that was essential to her. "This now makes us different from any other," she said, "and we will show the world our quiddity."

He figured that their *quiddity* meant their unique essence, and when she confirmed this, he ached with satisfaction.

The rest of that morning was spent relaxing and reading. Gideon found it hard to keep his concentration on the old English daily paper he was trying to read as he watched the Greek beauty bend, spin around, smile at him and just generally radiate over that boat.

"Tell me more about the Butterfly opera thing," he said, losing all interest in his paper.

"Thing?" she said. "You'll be saying 'and stuff' next, agápi mou!" She looked at her oversized wristwatch and said, "Midday, the sun is over the yard arm, sailor boy!" and she poured two glasses of white wine and selected a long-playing disc from a rack. "I'm putting the Humming Chorus on again as it affected you so deeply last time. I know you need to see the whole opera now, but let's get into the passion!" He couldn't argue with that.

She talked of the singers in the choir and their return to using individual syllables or vowel sounds to show the flexibility and control of their pitch and tone. "But now in a fragmented form. Those instruments darling, those weeping violas, clarinets and horns along with the gentle harp, with their vocal parts now slowing as if they were tiring, and then rising gently to the soft part called a *pianissimo,* to that high B flat. The chorus ends in an ethereal B flat major chord. Perfectly wonderful. It's too much to take in, I know. Just pick out the parts that you understand, I will teach you the rest over time."

She was right, Gideon could not take in all the information. But she had placed that seed, that earnest enthusiasm within him, and he watched her facial expressions change with those chords.

When the Humming Chorus crescendoed that day, a teardrop fell and slithered down her iced wine glass. Gideon watched its journey until it came to a gentle stop. She slowly twisted the glass from the stem and the drop edged onwards another eighth of an inch at a slightly different angle and finally came to a halt. An artistic, beautiful moment.

Chapter Twenty-Seven

The storm cometh

On the Monday morning, Gideon walked up and over the gangway to pull his station card out and chatted to the Quartermaster, who was Jazz that day.

He pulled Gideon closer. "Jeeze, you smell lovely, Gids. I hope she's as beautiful as she smells?"

Mr Hinkley appeared. He said to the Quartermaster, "You should move ship's company personnel away from the gangway as soon as you can, Leading Seaman Jasiewicz. It gives off a bad show to have them loitering."

Jazz was firm and in control. "No it doesn't, Sir and this is not how we operate on the Fighting Fifteen. Can I ask you Sir, have you any, and I mean *any* fucking idea what time of year this is?"

Gideon started to walk across the flight deck to drop down through the mortar well to go below. He stopped, turned and said to Jazz, "That's the problem with someone who honestly believes other cultures are inferior to our own. Their beliefs affect everything they say and do!"

It wasn't a great stab and his newfound language, but what made him swell with pride was that, without thinking, he was now half-quoting Xanthe.

Jazz walked up to Gideon and whispered, "Fuck off below, matey, I'll sort this pig out." He slapped Gideon on the arse as he disappeared down the railed ladder.

Down in the mess deck, Gideon found Mickey. "I figure you've already had a special Christmas, seeing as you are still lit up like a firework! We best have a beer then, my fine-smelling friend."

"But it's half past seven in the morning, on a warship."

"I know, Gids. Should have started earlier, but no matter…" Mickey laughed like a hyena and everything was alright again. "Don't concern yourself with that short-arsed

126

little fucker neither, not today," he added. "We'll sort that twat out soon enough with his arrogant zeal to catch you out!"

"How can you be so sure, Mick?"

"He's not following the rules. He's a low-ranking officer, but he thinks his background makes him special. Give a man enough rope…" and he tailed off with a nod and a wink.

Things soon escalated in the British withdrawal from Malta. In December 1971, after many negotiations, the Maltese Government demanded eleven million pounds immediately or the British must be off their lands by the 31st, leaving only six days remaining.

The British saw this as an unreasonable request. The upshot was that there was to be an immediate escalation of the withdrawal when the British carrier arrived. However, to their credit, the Maltese had negotiated a seven-year lease to wind down with practicality and dignity. Gideon had always observed that the Maltese people were good, loyal friends and very pro-British. This was a win-win situation for both parties, he thought.

HMS Bulwark, the Commando carrier moored between two buoys in the centre of Grand Harbour in mid-January. She took control of the withdrawal and most of the duties of the Euryalus crew, working with HMS St Angelo to escalate the operation. A code name was heard for the first time twenty-four hours after Bulwark arrived: 'Operation Exit' had officially started.

This left the crew of the Euryalus to do funny little tasks like filling in, driving, picking up personnel and guarding the armoury in St Angelo. This worked well for Gideon as he was on a day on, day off rota, which gave him plenty of free time to disappear.

The next day Gideon met Xanthe in a dusty bar in Luqa, where her friend Melanie was billeted. He mentioned the spat with Mr Hinkley and she talked of 'eager rivalry' that then escalates. "Boys will be boys and the female species can be as wicked too, trust me. But, gentle you, this emulation has turned into a hate with a zeal that goes beyond the call of duty."

Gideon had never come across meanness like Hinkley's. Firstly, there was no need for these emotions and secondly, he thought they all pulled together in the service? He began to really dislike him, a feeling he had not had before. "Lucky you!" Xanthe said, "Your first abhorrence at seventeen. I think that's probably a good thing." She added, "The main battle with the old order like Mr Hinkley is that they are sclerotic. This means that they become rigid, as in sclerosis, and lose the ability to adapt and harmonise."

How eloquently put, he thought. Even under deep scrutiny and with her career at risk, here she was being poetic and teaching him words. God, he loved her so. "You're good, lady. No, truly, you are good!" he said and kissed her perfumed neck.

Gozo had become their secret, untouched Mediterranean destination with its quaint villages, tiny, narrow streets, rustic bars and restaurants and craggy coves and cliffs where time seemed to slow to a crawl.

It was easy for them to blend in there and finding boltholes in the deserted streets and ancient bars became exciting and fun. Gideon also fell in love with staying in, sipping wine, chatting, learning and dipping in the pool for a swim in the warm night air; it was just as appealing as going out.

Sitting there one time in the quite evening air, she started to tell a story. "The other afternoon, I went to the funeral of a friend on the island. Over a drink at the wake, I walked up to the bereaved husband and said, 'Could I say a word?' He said, 'Yes, of course.' So I said to him, 'Plethora' and he said, 'Thanks, that means a lot.'" Xanthe fell about laughing.

Although he didn't really get the joke at first because *plethora* meant nothing to him, Gideon knew why she laughed so loudly – it must be funny to educated folk! He thought that if we all had a pleasure-seeking teacher looking like a Greek goddess, who gave us wine, slept naked next to us and made us feel unbelievably special, we would all learn what we should have learned at school! He was laughing too as he held her close, kissed her forehead and inhaled her very essence.

One pleasant afternoon, Xanthe and Gideon were on a roof-top veranda drinking champagne and laughing about old English stupidity. They were off the beaten track, which was not hard as most folk did not leave Valletta and the surrounding towns, because there were no amenities to speak of. They were looking down at a small paved area where people were drinking quietly.

Xanthe could 'read him,' and far from being spooked, he liked this very much indeed. It meant that she was always thinking of him, always ready to talk, guide and please him in every way possible. She could see now that he had something to say.

"I absolutely love how you have a story about everything," he said. "I mean there is always a link to history, mythology or some sweet-sounding word that you can trace and slip into a space. I just cannot imagine life without you. Oh, and there's something I've been wondering. Can you tell me about your name?"

"Ah! There is a story that goes with my name, curious boy. Well, my father desperately wanted two boys, so he couldn't think of a girl's name. Grandmamma came up with my name eventually, which was initially Ianthe. Do you know the story of Ianthe and Iphis?"

"Not a clue, Ma'am!" Of course, he knew he could never match the depth of her classical education, but he loved the fact that she could see in his expression that he was swept away by it all.

He looked at her seriously now. He needed to ask her something like, 'How will this end up?' or 'How can we ever stop this now?' Then Xanthe said, without any prompting, "I will work this out, dearest boy. If I have to leave the service, then so be it. But I will work something out. I think we are being followed. Look down there – in the red velvet jacket."

Before he could answer, she stood up in a fury and took his hand and they descended the spiral staircase to the paved area below. She looked around, staring hard at people and then walked towards a diminutive figure in an absurdly large fedora hat.

Still holding Gideon's hand, she tapped the man on the shoulder and as he turned around, she said to him, "You, Sir, are jealous of what we have."

Mr Hinkley look shocked.

She turned to Gideon and cried as she spoke. "He continually jabs at you and is jealous of all your hopes and dreams. He can't see those emotions and couldn't get them out of a paper bag if he wanted to and now he wants to put you down to his idea of where someone like you should be. And this is the horrible part, he wants to keep you there forever." She sobbed on, "You, beautiful you, fantastic you with your ebullience and youth. That man wants to drag you down to where he is in his loneliness. Christ, misery loves company and here it is acting out on the stage of life, with him the protagonist and you the unwilling servant!"

The initial sneering pleasure on Hinkley's face was now disappearing as he tried to decipher what she had just said to him.

How authoritative Xanthe looked in her rage against the destroyer! Gideon stood next to her with his muscled arm around her waist. Her silver jewellery glistened in the sun, bright against the hue of her skin. The soft grey and white feather that she had worn on that red-sand beach was now flapping in her left ear, making her look like a movie star. Clearly, this had an effect on Mr Hinkley, who looked her boldly up and down.

Gideon looked him straight into the eye. "You are a fucking arsehole, Sir!"

Xanthe grabbed Gideon's hand and they ran down to the craggy waterfront. She was crying and kissing him. The waves were suddenly agitated and as the spindrift rose, Xanthe stared out to sea. She whispered; "Kymopoleia. Christ, what have I just done?"

"You, *we*, did the right thing, my love," Gideon said. "I'll protect you. I promise."

What had Hinkley done, he thought? How could he have endangered everything? After all that had happened, they simply could not be apart. But how could they stay together after this?

He looked at her and could see she knew it too. The storm was finally coming.

Chapter Twenty-Eight

The Sword of Damocles

The rest of that afternoon was tense and nothing like what they had become used to. They took a taxi back to the White Mansions in silence. When they arrived, Gideon paid the driver and as they stood there, and she sobbed inconsolably. She kissed him passionately and held his face with both hands, whispering, "You must go, agápi mou, I will work something out. Truly." With that, she ran up the steps to her accommodation.

He walked a little and then hailed another taxi. Later, he clambered on board the Euryalus a frightened individual.

The next morning Gideon was piped to the Regulating Office, where the kind and gentle Master-at-Arms said that there was transport waiting to take him to St Andrew's Barracks. He said with genuine warmth, "Hold your own, lad!"

The ride there was in silence and Gideon entered the building where he met the same two investigating officers that were there the first time. Good guy, bad guy.

The good cop asked what had he to say for himself.

Gideon held it together and said, "I love her so, so much, Sir, that it hurts. I am in an incredible place, no matter what happens to me now. She put me there and I would not have missed this opportunity for all the tea in China. Sir." It was a shitty description, he thought, but it was all he could come up with at that moment.

Bad cop huffed and walked out. Confession over and all that. Got his man! What!

"What would you like to happen now then, young man?" the Army Major said. He walked around from behind his desk and sat on the corner of it, gesturing for Gideon to sit down. He offered him a cigarette, which he accepted and once it was lit, he inhaled deeply with relief. Strange, as he didn't smoke cigarettes, but it seemed like the natural thing to do.

Some of the questions that followed were unanswerable except that Gideon wanted to be with her forever, no matter what the consequences. He tailed off into a pathetic, head-shaking emptiness.

The gentle Major said, "You are a young man and the type we need desperately in the services and there is something about you that we like, so this what is going to happen …" Gideon heard nothing after that though he had an overwhelming feeling that he was being let off, because this was a court-martial offence in the Navy.

Gideon asked if he could see Xanthe again and to his surprise, the kind Major said with a sigh and a gesture of his hand, "Of course." His cigarette smoke spiralled towards the deck-head fan in slow motion before being whisked away by the quiet turning blades.

"What happens now, Sir?" Gideon croaked.

The Major said with an odd smile that he was an old-fashioned romantic and had relished the chase, but now, having cornered the fox, "I'm having the over-riding thought of helping the creature to escape. 0800 lad, no dramas, eh? We know where to find her. She knows this of course."

It was a kind gesture, an offer. The Major didn't have to help Gideon in any way.

It was the Navy that would punish him, but here at St Andrew's Barracks, there were both Army and Marine personnel in this Special Investigation Unit. Undeniably, this was an inter-service rivalry: the Army officer disliked the fact that the Marine officer had no time for a bottom feeder like Gideon. This was why he wanted to intervene, and Gideon was given transportation back to St Angelo.

On board, Mickey was there with rum in the Quarterdeck locker. "I ain't heard nothing like it, Nipper. I've been in over fifteen years and you've bagged the Golden Chalice under a dog watch! I think you'll be OK if that Brown Job is genuine, but Miss X? They're gonna fucking hang her out to dry, Gids!"

"What's a dog watch, Mick, in your context?"

Later, Gideon met Xanthe on the boat named 'T L Sea,' and immediately he knew something was different within her. He told her of his meeting with the Intelligence Service and she said that she knew because she had been there, too.

"What happens to us?" he said pathetically and she came out with a bottle of iced Sancerre, which they drank in silence in chipped glass tooth mugs. It had never tasted better.

After that wine and some Greek cheese and olives, Xanthe said that she had to report to the Special Investigation Unit again in the morning for an alleged offence of misconduct unbecoming of an officer. She was being picked up from the boat. She was upset and shocked, but could Gideon detect a note of acceptance in her tone too?

She held his hands across the small table and said: "I have lived under the Sword of Damocles and now it has fallen on me. I knew the deleterious consequences of our relationship, darling. Always remember how we started and how beautiful our journey has been. And will be!"

Intimacy had never been more tender-hearted than it was that night. She cried during orgasm and shouted: "This will never be over!" Afterwards, as he lay there in her scented arms, Xanthe said, "You are so young and helpless. I will come and get you. I promise with all my being."

Gideon was filled with a warmth of belonging as she gently rocked him to sleep.

At around 0400 in the morning, he awoke, perspiring from every pore. He got up and sat on the edge of the bed to look at her flat stomach gently moving up and down. He blinked his eyes in a childish attempt to simulate a camera shutter so that his memory would never lose this image.

The rhythmic ticking of the brass nautical wall clock clicked mellifluously in his ears and brought a warm memory of his childhood. When she woke, she sat up with a smile, looked him straight in the eye and whispered:

"Keep believing in me. I will come and get you."

She looked tearful and Gideon's heart was making his stomach churn, but her words encouraged him because she had said 'get' and not just 'find.' They made love as if the world was going to end, as indeed it did for them that sultry morning.

The light was changing and making the bay sparkle like a polychromatic dream. Inside, the room looked like an old brown photograph in the stillness of the dawn.

Xanthe could not hide her emotions as she sat staring out to sea. She lifted a book called *Grand Central* something. She quoted, "Your love will be my perpetual warmth, agápi mou. I wanted to find that quote for you." She added, "I kiss your soul," and kissed him.

They watched the sun come up over the horizon and Gideon licked the saltiness from her cheeks.

There was a beep-beep from a military Land Rover on the quay. Gideon whispered, "I have to go, I can't, I don't want to but...?"

Her eyes revealed a tortured soul and she said looking into his, "I *will* come and get you Gideon, and bring you home!"

He could see two Royal Marines, the Euryalus Master-at-Arms and another high-ranking Wren waiting on the jetty. There was no Hollywood-style running up the rickety gangplank or military shouting. This small, kind act was England at her stiff-upper-lipped best, he supposed.

Through her tears she cried; "*S'agapo*, I love you so much and my blindness has destroyed us. I'm so very sorry my beautiful, beautiful boy, agóri... no one will ever take your place."

Gideon broke away from her and drank down the last of the wine from last evening. As he tried to leave, she had a finger in his waistband and was tugging, a tender but futile gesture. She bit her bottom lip, flashing those dark Greek eyes.

The moment was surreal. Her last words were, "Soon, I'll get us out of the Hadal Zone. I promise."

He walked down the gangway. The Master said; "Off you go then, lad" in an avuncular way and he saw the Marine's look that said, 'Really sorry, mate. This shouldn't be happening.' The expression on the female Officer's face, though, was one of abhorrence.

Gideon turned around and Xanthe was staring at him, her white kimono with its red, floral leitmotif billowing in the gentle breeze. She mouthed, "I love you so much," before the two Marines ascended the gangway to detain her. Gideon turned and ran down to the square to get a cab. As a morning breeze cooled his face, he felt like calling out to Aeolus: *do something!*

Chapter Twenty-Nine

The Hadal Zone

Back on board the Euryalus, everything was blank in Gideon's eyes. He was like a snake that had shed its skin: suddenly grown up. He felt as if he had been given an inner calm, but nothing had prepared him for the pain and sorrow.

HMS Euryalus sailed from Malta in February of the New Year and they headed back home via Sicily, Naples and Palma in Mallorca; the bluest of the blue periods he had ever known. The crew kept him buoyant and entertained and educated him, even though nobody on the lower deck except Mickey knew of his heartbreak.

Sub-Lieutenant Hinkley was no longer on board. Gideon knew that he was meant to stay with the ship until they arrived in the UK as the sea training whilst steaming back would have been beneficial and a 'jolly' for him too. Gideon asked Mickey about this.

"I am under instructions to keeps this under my hat, Gids. However, you are a decent lad and I believe you have the right to know some of it. He has been drafted off the ship and reassigned to duties appertaining to a cunt!" They laughed like children do at a rude joke.

"We look after our own, matey, even the knobs in the Wardroom are part of the team. Never forget that, eh? Hinkley's in line for some minor title and he has to do four years in the Navy like our Royals do, so the Fighting Fifteen has stamped that card for him."

No matter what had happened between Xanthe and Gideon, it seemed that Mr Hinkley had broken the silent, unwritten naval code of ethics. "Probity is alive and kicking!" Mickey said.

The first port of call was Naples, and this was Gideon's first time in Italy, but he didn't find anything romantic, mysterious or wonderful as most folk did, even though the touristy bits were unique and the history awesome. His heart was bleak and strangely, surrounded by the crew, he was lonely.

Upon arrival, the Captain of the Euryalus, with his plummy voice, asked over the tannoy system if the crew would make a special show in the ceremonial entrance to the busy harbour as there was a huge American presence there controlling the Mediterranean NATO fleet.

As they entered Naples Harbour, the first ship they would pass was the USS Yellowstone, a massive Samuel Gompers class vessel built in the 1960s. It was important, as it was a floating office and Communication Centre with lots of high-ranking NATO officers on board.

Gideon and Bomber were on the bridge deck head as the piping party, so they had the best position to view this magnificent scene and all the pomp and ceremony that goes with such an entrance.

"Stand by to pipe the still!" screamed the Chief Gunnery Instructor, playing a role that surely deserved a crack at an Oscar. He added quietly to the pair of them, "Now don't fuck it all up, lads." Of course they wouldn't – they had done this kind of entrance dozens of times. It was just a shrill from a Bosun's Call.

The Yellowstone returned their salute and over their upper deck loudspeaker system announced without irony, "Attention to port! HMS You're-all-arse" and everybody on the Euryalus fell about like rag dolls in a wind tunnel. Gideon had to pipe the 'Carry on' in return, but it was too late. It sounded like budgerigars drunk on rum trying to blow the Bosun's Call underwater. England and America at their finest, showing the world why the bad guys will never win, as Mickey said later after berthing.

Palma was very impressive with its massive Santa María Cathedral, a Gothic landmark begun in the 13th century which overlooks the Bay of Palma, but Gideon felt companionless, devastated and barren of mind, despite the perks of sailing the Mediterranean.

The Euryalus headed for Devonport for a period of

essential maintenance. The ship was then detailed up to the Arctic Circle to take part in a sabre-rattling exercise as the second "Cod War" with Iceland loomed. They were at constant battle stations in heavy seas and this situation wasn't going anywhere. That pretty much described Gideon's heart too. Mickey was his saviour in all this: kind, crude, funny, and philosophical as ever.

They were sitting in the Quarterdeck locker when the temperature was well below zero and the sea raged outside. The compartment was festooned with ropes, marlin spikes, paintbrushes and all the nautical fittings of the life of a seaman and Mickey was showing Gideon how to make a Monkey's Fist. This was a knot of magical proportions and was made quickly with modern ropes to amuse kids at parties or people who had seen everything right up until that particular knot. Mickey said, "I'll teach you how to make one of these with one hand whilst rolling a cigarette in the other and you will not need to take a bird's knickers off because they will be on the deck already. Now look lively and pay a-fucking-tention!"

Gideon was staring into space and Mick said, "We had better get you laid quickly, my little friend. She can have your heart, but I need your dopey, loved-up head!"

Now there is a man's man, Gideon thought. Crude and outdated, but kind and honest towards his young ward. "Do you know what the metaphor is if you quote the Sword of Damocles, Mick?" he asked.

Mickey finished the knot he was tying and closed one eye as the smoke from his cigarette stung it. He inhaled the smoke and exhaled loudly. "I forget the fucker's name, son. Let me think… Damocles, yeah yeah. He was a sycophantic swanker in King something or other's court. I think? Yeah! For sure. The King was fed up with Damocles sniffing up his arse and thinking a king's job was easy, so he invited him to scran but hung a fucking great sword above his head, held only by a human hair. The thing is, it was to point out… well, the precariousness of his position, being in charge and stuff and how fucking shite it was sometimes! Why do you ask, matey?"

"How do *know* all this stuff?" Gideon croaked through tears of laughter.

"Because, my rollicking, bollocking Son of Neptune, I read books too! She said you two were under the Sword of Damocles, did she? She must have loved you beyond the pale. Fuck me ol' brown boots!" He shook his head in wonderment. "What has she done to you, my friend?"

The Euryalus berthed back in Devonport for essential maintenance in the dockyard and the crew had summer leave before the Icelandic situation became full-blown. Within those four months, the second 'Cod War' had commenced.

Part of Gideon's instruction was about basic Oceanography. As a submarine hunter, he had to learn why their sonar emissions were bent by the depth of the sea and the various amounts of salinity it contained, as this had an effect on the range predictions.

On the bulkhead of the Sonar Control Room, there was a childlike chart of the four named depths of the ocean, and as he looked up at it, he realised that he had never really taken any notice of it at all. He stood up and touched the word *Epipelagic* (from the surface down to around 660 feet), slid his digit down to *Mesopelagic* (further down to 3,300 feet), known as the Twilight Zone. Some light penetrates this depth, he read, but insufficient for photosynthesis. *Bathypelagic* was next, a familiar word. He had accompanied Mickey in Storm Force Eights to put a Bathythermograph into a launcher over the stern, to predict ranges prior to transmitting. By this depth (13,100 feet), the ocean is almost entirely dark.

Then of course, the *Abyssopelagic* (19,700 feet) down to and above the ocean floor. No light whatsoever penetrates to this depth. The name is derived from the Greek *abyss*, meaning bottomless, infinite. How apt, he thought.

Then finally, a fifth layer: the trenches that go deeper, the *Hadopelagic*. The name, he knew, was derived from *Hades*, the classical Greek underworld. He spread his palm over the word and his heart filled with joy. Her last words to him had included the words Hadal Zone. It all made sense now.

A Petty Officer walked into the Sonar Control Room and snapped, "What are you doing, you little shit? Fucking daydreaming again? Get sweeping, it's what you bottom feeders do!" He smiled and winked at Gideon as he disappeared back into the Operations Room.

The Hadal Zone. It certainly felt as though he was there. And the Sword of Damocles. She knew the risk and still took it. Thankfully. He thought back to Xanthe bringing up Socrates too. "The only true wisdom is in knowing you know nothing, agápi mou!" she had said. Well, he knew that in matters of the heart, he was beyond repair. Where was she? He just knew in his heart that she would come and get him.

Operational commitments continued for him and the duties never eased. There was at that time a mass scaling back of bases overseas and many outdated personnel whose skills were sadly now redundant were put out to grass, but new ships were still being built and they needed to be manned so that obligations could be met.

Gideon started to read Greek mythology. As Xanthe had warned, it was all so serious and difficult to read. He was annoyed with the authors as the hundreds of stories which had such depth and meaning were written for more highly educated folk. He could see that to dumb down the myths for the masses might infringe on their territory of these elite, but surely the myths were for everyone? Xanthe had taught him to chase after knowledge with his natural curiosity and yet he now found a barrier.

The punishment Gideon received for his time with Xanthe was to be drafted to the Leviathan, HMS Bulwark. He had expressed his fear of serving on such a beast while in Malta and did so again when the dreaded chit was handed to him. His heart was heavy as he walked up her gangway.

However, the crew were all amazing in their individual ways and Gideon came to love the day-to-day life of a floating city, a ship that never slept.

Bulwark went straight out to Cyprus to land a Commando Unit. Rest and recreation in Athens was painful for Gideon. He had bought a map of Greece and sprawled it over a table trying to work out how to get to the town of Nafplion. Xanthe said she had a house there and it was a two-hour drive from where he was. He knew this was futile as what would he do if he got there? And he had no driving licence anyway, although everyone said hiring a car was easy. The problem, they all said, was getting out of the city. Gideon was upset with frustration and felt helpless. The crew prescribed alcohol for this condition.

Why hadn't Xanthe come and found him? She had known that in Gideon's position, it would be impossible for him to come to her. He had total belief that she would still come. She would be working on a solution, he was certain, but he couldn't help feeling abandoned.

Chapter Thirty

Yuliana

They sailed out of the Mediterranean and up to Rotterdam to embark Dutch Marines. Then across to North Carolina to drop some of that unit there and then down to Fort Lauderdale, Florida, where the main unit would hook up with Americans to prevent drug smuggling operations from finding a gateway into Miami.

The ship was then sent to Cartagena in Colombia, for rest and recreation but also as a show of force to the population, letting them know that joint forces were in the area to suppress a growing international problem.

Gideon went ashore with a good buddy, Jerry, a naval Writer, which was naval terminology for a clerk, and Paul, a Radar Plotter, a big Cornishman. They hailed a cab and Paul pleaded for the driver to, "Take us to a bad area where there are naughty women, my friend." The driver rolled his eyes, crossed himself and drove off with a toothless smile. The boys liked him very much and without asking his name, they called him José.

They arrived at what looked like a seedy bar in the seedy area of Getsemani. The surroundings, however, were pleasant and comfortable, with strange characters all looking either scared or overly pleased with themselves. Paul figured this was the right place to be.

A 'receptionist' at the bar asked what the boys were looking for, the duration required and what needs and fetishes they might have. Paul said just, "Fat and anal" and went to sit down, much to their amusement. He was, Gideon thought, like an overweight Mickey.

Jerry had a specific list. Long hair, voluptuous and 'a bit of a temper.' They all thought from what they had seen in the movies that they were in the right place for that.

It had been seven months since he had parted from

Xanthe, and Gideon just wanted release. Jerry and Paul were paired off with attractive girls and all three arranged to meet in the Cantina across the road in an hour or so.

Instead of being introduced to a girl, Gideon was shown to an office upstairs with a veranda open to the city's magic street noises below. A beautiful older lady called Isabella asked him to sit down and gave him another beer from her fridge. "Your needs are different, aren't they?" she said. "Normal, but different." Gideon wanted to back out. Masturbation was all the relief he needed now. "Antonella says you want relief, and that's easy, but I don't think you are the quick jerking off type? Trust me, I know. So, in two sentences, tell me what makes you, well... you?"

Goodness me, Gideon thought, I am in a bordello in South America and I am being treated with kindness, as if by a psychoanalyst.

"Easy, Ma'am. The Navy cruelly took away the one true love I've ever had. I feel I'm betraying her, but... she's not coming back right now. I have to find relief without affecting my heart. I hope she would understand?"

"How long would you need this girl for?" she said.

"Four minutes, Ma'am," he said without hesitation.

"Oh dear, oh dear!" she said with a very heavy Spanish accent. "I have a proposition for you. Special girl and a one-off price for the whole week..." She went on to say something about a girl they were especially fond of called Yuliana... but all he could hear in his head was a Greek accent telling him that she loved him.

A young lady was brought to Gideon in a private room next to Isabella's office. She looked his age and was a mestizo, of mixed race and great beauty. "This is Yuliana," he was told.

He went to pay his pesos to Isabella next door and she smiled with a knowing look. He had paid her well over what she had asked and rounded up to the nearest hundred. He said thank you, then as he was going through the door, turned around, walked back and kissed her on the cheek. She whispered, "I knew you were kind!" and he strode back into the room where Yuliana still stood.

He did not know how to proceed with this divine-looking person. As if she had read his thoughts, she grasped his hand and took him downstairs and out the back, where there were huts with straw roofs in a semi-circle around the rear of the compound.

They entered what turned out to be her cabin. It was clean and cool-looking in a Hawaiian way, and Gideon felt at ease. Yuliana lit two joints and opened two bottles of beer, gave Gideon one and then took her blouse and Levi's shorts off. She was now standing there in maroon laced underwear.

He toked on the joint, exhaled and took a sip of beer. He walked towards her and gently put his hand behind her neck with the thumb rubbing her jaw. He could feel the semen leaking from his penis inside his shorts.

"I do kissing," she said, sultry and teasing.

"Gosh, I hope so, but please, sit down, relax, this is good right now," he said. She did relax and they had forty-odd minutes of laughing and sussing each other out before they crossed the road to the Cantina.

Sure enough, they were joined by Paul, who looked at Yuliana and said, "Wow!" Five minutes later, Jerry arrived, said, "What the fuck is this?!" and they all laughed.

Yes, Gideon told them, he had acquired the company of the delightful pony-tailed Yuliana for five days and no, he had not slept with her. The tales Paul and Jerry told about the last sixty minutes were funny and outrageous, and Gideon was almost envious. However, they could not believe his luck and their wonderment and comments made him glad of his choice. This seemed to please Yuliana too.

The lads drifted off and Gideon had no idea what to do with this harmonious and desirable woman. "What would you like to do this afternoon?" he said when the conversation slowed. "I do kissing," she teased and smiled. "You want to fuck now?"

"No, let's go eat something. I want to get immersed in this crazy culture of yours, if that's OK?"

She clearly knew what he meant and her eyes lit up. He was fascinated by her, and she seemed to be responding to what he hoped was kindness. Perhaps she was not usually treated with manners and equality?

He asked her what Colombians ate so she talked excitedly non-stop for some minutes, as if a firework had lit up in front of him. He couldn't understand a word she was saying but found her enthusiasm charming.

She slowed down and he was able to understand that being biodiverse, her country was hard to beat when it came to cuisine. They ordered a meal and at first he had no idea what he was eating, apart from rice and some grilled steak. He spotted some pork rind and some kind of beans with a fried egg on top, which seemed bizarre to him. Sliced on top of that was avocado and banana which he really felt didn't mix. He picked out the bits he recognised, but felt like a philistine. He thought of the apricots in Xanthe's pasty.

It was all washed down with Aguardiente. This, she explained, was their national liquor, and he was impressed that they had such a thing. When he asked what the word meant, Yuliana said, "Burning water," which is what it tasted like to him.

They spent the afternoon drinking in bars around the old walled city, which was truly remarkable as there was no tourism. They walked into a clean, ordinary-looking hotel and Gideon paid for a room overlooking a colourful square. It looked like a calendar shot with all the bright colours, especially the ubiquitous mustard yellow. He had always loved the study of flags and thought that it was as if their national flag had been melted all over this area.

Yuliana pulled a couple of beers from the fridge and snapped them open. Gideon approached her again and went to put his hand around her neck to pull her towards him. She hesitated, a look of fright on her face. He pulled away in horror at the idea that she thought he would hurt her. He quickly figured that she was used to nice men suddenly becoming violent once they had gained her trust. He went to turn away and she stopped him and hugged him. Then she cried and cried.

Gideon held her for a long time, and then wiped her tears away. He lifted her up like a movie star, gently laid her on the bed and covered her over with a blanket. She was asleep before he sat down. He picked up his beer, smiled and thought, 'I'm not sleeping with you on the first date – you'll think I'm easy!' He laughed at his own silly thoughts.

He woke around five in the morning on the big L-shaped sofa with Yuliana sitting over his erect phallus. Her hair covered her whole face and she was wearing only his white shirt. He could not move as she vigorously rode up and down on him, and now she was beginning to moan.

The weed they had smoked had dulled his senses and although it was pleasurable beyond belief, he didn't feel himself wanting to ejaculate straight away, so she just kept pumping up and down on him. Waking up fully now, he held on to her hips and looked her into her eyes as she flipped that tsunami of hair off her face.

After many minutes, he had the release he had so desperately yearned for and she screamed, shuddered and came to a halt. She dismounted, and in the foetal position, snuggled into Gideon as they drifted back to sleep. The last words he heard from those bee-stung lips were, "I look after you."

Gideon tried to make the next five days the happiest of her life.

Chapter Thirty-One

So be it

The Bulwark sailed from Cartagena the following Monday to do a public relations exercise for a retiring Admiral off Virgin Gorda in the British Virgin Islands. They then re-engaged with the Dutch Marines on the island of Vieques and participated in a week's training, then sailed back to Fort Lauderdale where Gideon managed to call Yuliana. After a week alongside there, they sailed back south and berthed in Oranjestad in the Dutch Caribbean island of Aruba for a goodwill visit. Yuliana flew there to meet Gideon on a private island-hopper, having spoken at great length with him on that very troublesome phone connection between the two continents.

Yuliana had mentioned one evening in Cartagena that her Uncle Sebastián, her legal guardian, was something in a cartel. Her father was unknown and her mother had disappeared, so she was just left with this powerful relative. He had placed her in a brothel when he thought her age was around sixteen. This was of course shocking, but Gideon would observe that Uncle Sebastián still appeared to take his parental duties seriously, and he had seen how happy Yuliana was with Gideon.

When the Bulwark berthed in Oranjestad, Yuliana was there on the jetty looking like a glossy magazine cover model and waving like crazy at everybody. She told Gideon that her uncle had arranged her flight, which pleased and scared him at the same time. She had brought bags, she said, but they were left at the terminal building. He wondered what role she had played to get this flight?

As Gideon was detailed to work with the Naval Police, he had no duties involving the day-to-day running of the vessel, so he was free to go ashore when it was permissible. He was soon granted a seven-day leave pass.

At the time, Aruba was relativity drug-free and this had made it a haven for unscrupulous characters in transit from Venezuela to Columbia. The kindly uncle had a house here in the San Nicolas area south of the island, about eleven miles from the town, and Gideon and Yuliana were to stay there. It was a modern building built to fit in with the local area and not to draw too much attention. The gardens surrounding it were heavy with foliage, including many palms.

In the garage was a beaten-up 1954 Chevy 3100 Pick-up which they drove to get supplies. They were surprised that it started first time and sounded so throaty, so they looked under the hood and the mechanics were clean and new, with modern mufflers which, Gideon noted, had a timbre that only America vehicles could produce. It had to be a getaway vehicle, they pondered that evening as they toked on the uncle's finest cannabis. They laughed and made fantasy plans to rob a bank with it.

"I like the '54," Gideon said. "It was only in production for about eighteen months before they revamped it. That was a good year for everything, I think!" He smiled, because he was born that year.

"I want to be born in 1954 too," she said with her hands on her hips, charmingly determined. It turned out she had no idea when she was born and never knew her relatives apart from Uncle Sebastián.

That evening they stayed in, only needing each other. The weed, the alcohol and the sound of the cicadas helped though, they agreed. So Yuliana wanted to have a birth date? Teasing her gently, he said he would give it some thought.

They spent the next few days looking at the island and they particularly liked the rugged terrain around Arikok. The hilltops offer sweeping views and they rented horses and, after a quick lesson in a corral, they were good to go. Gideon's skills were rusty but she rode like a pro, laughing at him all the time. The wrangler figured she was good enough to look after a novice like Gideon and he was right.

Her smile was infectious and as he looked at her talking about the leaf-toed geckos endemic to this island and the unique iguanas sitting in trees or crossing their path, he wondered who she really was? But it didn't seem to matter and soon drifted from his mind.

They came to a ledge and Yuliana told him proudly that fifty per cent of all known species of lizard in the world live on Aruba. Also, she said that you could see Venezuela on a clear day from this viewpoint. Gideon shook his head in awe. "It's only fifty feet away," she laughed, and Gideon cared not a jot if it was inches, yards or furlongs. He just loved her whole being. She was smarter than him and he liked that.

As she was staring out to sea, he sat astride his horse behind her and wondered whether such a smart girl could reason with her guardian to get her away from her life at the brothel? He hated himself for thinking of it now. She seemed to be healing in this time away. Maybe her uncle had let her go and this was why she was so happy? He was to hang on to that thought for the rest of the week.

"You are quite bewitching, young lady," he said.

She turned her horse around and smiled as though she had won the Miss World title. "I don't know what that means, but I know it's beautiful, *el hombre*," she said in her lovely accent. Gideon knew that *el hombre* in this context meant 'lover,' and this pleased him.

Back in their accommodation, they changed outfits and she seemed pensive and unable to relax. Facing her, it was hard to hide his erection in his Bermuda shorts, as she was in her bikini with her ample breasts moving with the rhythm of her breathing.

"Your lips taste like nectar," he said, "which makes me wonder what the rest of you might taste like?"

She burst out laughing and threw her arms around him. They kissed passionately and made gentle, meaningful love on the circular bed, with all the doors and windows open. The fan was slow-moving and a pair of geckos scampered up the wall as the sea crashed onto the nearby beach. She went to say something urgently, but he put his finger across her lips and slowly shook his head from side to side. Whatever it was, he told her, it didn't matter right then. He wanted to say something to her too, but it could all wait.

The days continued to be as lovely as that one. He especially loved the floating tray in the pool carrying a breakfast of croissants, fruit and beer. It was sublime, as if Yuliana and that exotic island were holding together his broken heart.

After many weeks of working closely with Americans in the Caribbean, the ship berthed back in Fort Lauderdale. Gideon hired a car and drove to meet Yuliana at Miami Airport. There she was at the terminal with her long, fulsome hair scrunched up into a ponytail and pulled through the back of her baseball cap. She wore brilliant white pumps and frayed denim shorts. Her eyes burned into his and she seemed like a different person from the one he had first met.

Gideon was soon to be deeply involved with the prevention of Class A drugs moving into Miami from Columbia, yet here she was, a product of everything the UK and America stood against. Because in all probability, she was now working for the bad guys.

They stayed on South Beach in an Art Deco hotel where her uncle had a suite. Gideon thought it couldn't be bad being a gangster if you could afford a suite like this. Yuliana said that locals called this area *So-Be*. He liked that and quipped, "Ah! So be it!" The stuffy English phrase fell flat of course.

The area was impoverished, with a very high crime rate. There was a mix of Spanish speaking peoples: the Mexican Spanish, the Cuban Spanish and many more, as dozens of variants had arrived in this port in Florida. Yuliana pointed out that there were differences on many levels, but she could still tell where a Hispanic person came from by certain words and by their accents.

Over cold beer and spliffs, they talked and talked, especially about her promotion. Her uncle had not allowed her to go back to work at the bordello, and it would appear that she was now a representative of the cartel. She didn't say as much, but Gideon figured that she was a courier. It wasn't fighter-pilot school to work out where she got the *ganga* they were now smoking.

After intense copulation and still naked, Gideon said, "You should just pick a day for your birthday." She sat up, intrigued. "It's just a way to take your place in first-world society. Not that you need to fit in anywhere, special lady."

"Special? I love it! I love that special lady thing!" she said. "I would like you to pick me a date, lover!" Although she was slightly older than him, Gideon decided that she was born in 1954, the same year as him, and of course, that wonderful Chevy in Aruba.

So now they shared the same birthday: the 12th of March 1954, which delighted her. She couldn't believe that she actually had a birth date.

The week was amazing for both of them, but parting was sorrowful and inconclusive.

"I will write to you," she said. "Keep in touch and I will come to you, I promise, Gideon, with all my heart." It was, he thought with an aching heart, the second time someone had said they would come and get him.

And she did write. The letters would arrive full of tales of the fast life she was now living and always professing her love for Gideon.

After arriving back in the UK, Gideon was promoted to Leading Seaman, the same rank as his erstwhile hero, Mickey. A year after Miami, he was on another Leander class frigate, sailing for torpedo trials off Andros in the Bahamas where he was due to meet with Yuliana later in Nassau.

Although the scenery was magical, the work was boring and repetitive and yet they all managed in their own way to alleviate the boredom of being closed up in the Sonar Control Room with their different hopes and dreams. They were monitoring and recording ranges, depths and all other aspects of oceanography as torpedoes were launched by the

British and watched by the Americans. This went on for four weeks before they were allowed R & R in Nassau in the Bahamas.

Ashore on Paradise Island in Nassau, Gideon was drinking quietly when his fellow sailors pointed out a heavily moustached man who was watching him. This stranger was wearing an expensive white suit, looked like a celebrity and had an air of confidence, Gideon thought, looking his way in between slurps from his straw.

Gideon was intrigued and walked over to front him up, albeit in a pleasant way. Before he could say anything, the suit quickly gestured for him to sit down and apologised for staring. "I had to know which one was Gideon," he said. "Please, will you have a drink?"

Gideon wasn't going to turn down a drink and asked for a Mojito. The white suit ordered two and they chatted about pleasantries. The man introduced himself as José and said that the firm he worked for had asked him to find Gideon on this island.

"Why?" he asked, intrigued.

Jose pulled out a photograph and slid it across the table. It showed the head and shoulders of a female cadaver, covered in blood. The ashen face was swollen and purple with bruising and it looked as though it had been quickly wiped off and her tousled hair pulled into some sort of style. But dead she was, lying on a steel table. This girl had been pretty, Gideon could tell. But he had no idea why he was being shown her picture.

Jose spoke softly. "A significant client of the firm I represent tried to fuck this lady even though she was not working in that trade by then. When she refused, he tried to rape her. She shot and killed him with his own gun and his bodyguards shot her in retaliation. That's what caused the severe lacerations and disfigurement of the face."

Indeed, Gideon could see now where bullets had gone through that once gorgeous face.

"I'm sorry for the loss, for someone anyway," he said rather feebly, not knowing where this was going.

"It is Yuliana," José said, and Gideon went numb. "Sebastián needed you to know she died with her honour intact, Señor. The pig that did this and his close associates are no longer with us, I can assure you. Sebastián asked me to extend my hand and say to you that you were the only man to treat her as she deserved. Her heart was your heart and now it's his heart. Because of this, I am to invite you back to Cartagena when you are ready, Señor. If it takes two or whatever years, then so be it. She loved saying 'So be it' at the end of everything. That's you in her, my friend, isn't it?"

Gideon's eyes filled at the mention of 'So be it.' He had thought that phrase had fallen flat with Yuliana and he could not contain his tears any more.

This kind man stood up, picked up the photograph and put it in his pocket. He placed his hand on Gideon's shoulder, gave him a business card, then squeezed his shoulder and walked away. The card just said *José* and then there was a very long Columbian number.

Gideon sat alone in shock and drank both Mojitos while he tried to compose himself. He must have been sitting there for twenty minutes when his good buddy, a huge Welshman called David, came up to his table. He was flushed with rum and looking like a cartoon character.

"Fucking hell, Moo, we thought you'd got lost. What's with that nonce then?" he said in his broad Welsh accent.

"Nobody. Mistaken identity and all that." What could he say? A beautiful woman had fallen in love with him and her uncle was a drug runner and had sent this man to see if he wanted to be in the family now, as she had been murdered by bodyguards defending the rapist piece of shit that she had shot and killed? The tears wouldn't stop coming.

"Come on, Moo, cocktails to drink and pretty girls to ogle!" said the big lump of lovable Welsh lard as they walked back to the party, his protective arm around Gideon.

To explain his tear-stained state, Gideon told his friends that he was not the one that the suit was looking for, but it had made him sad because it made him think of Cartagena.

'Dinger' Bell, a snappy dresser and a man of twisted wit said, "Stop burbling, Moo! What the fuck are you going on about? What really went on with you in South America with all this mestizo shite? Second thoughts, we don't wanna know!"

Everyone fell about laughing but Gideon had sunk back down to the Hadal Zone for the second time in his life.

Chapter Thirty-Two

Elysian Fields

In 1984, Gideon was now thirty years old, and it had been twelve years since he had parted with Xanthe and she had still not shown up. His saudade was deeper than ever and destroying his relationships, he knew. Gideon decided to go to work himself and track her down. He could not believe she would have given up on him. Something had clearly gone wrong.

He went first to Crete on leave as she had said in the boat that day that they must get to Knossos. He remembered it clearly: her laying there, her hand on her stomach as she said it. He figured that would be a good start before the longer shot of going to Nafplion.

He stayed in a complex on the hilltop overlooking Mirabello Bay in Elounda. He made good friends immediately with the owner. This wonderful Greek character was a wily old anti-European called Vangelis, with a rather serious German wife.

The first jasmine-filled evening with the mellifluous cicadas charming his senses along with the ice-cold Greek beer, Gideon told Vangelis his tale of love. He shared almost every detail about his Greek lady in this drunken male bonding session and he had the warmest of responses from both his host and Ann, his wife, who was within earshot. He was received with a sympathetic, passionate ear.

The next morning, as they nursed their hangovers beside the pool, Vangelis informed Gideon that he had some news about his 'broken heart.'

Because Gideon had said that Xanthe was a proud Thessalonian, Vangelis had contacted cousins of his in England. Although Christodoulou was a common Greek surname, he had been told of a family with that name who indeed had had a daughter called Xanthe. Gideon was astounded.

"Her family were reasonably easy to find in London," Vangelis beamed. "They only had to go to Wood Green and St Mary's Greek Orthodox Church. Start talking about family in such a place and you will get a very strong feeling of this culture and our loyalties."

Gideon could not believe how smooth, easy and quick it had been for these kind folk. Sadly, the lady they had tracked down, the mother of the said Xanthe, had shuffled off this mortal coil and there was no information about the daughter. What they had learned though, was that there was a sibling of the daughter who was left behind in Thessaloniki when she moved to England, and he was still alive in that city.

"Would you like a cold beer, my young friend, to kill that hangover?" Vangelis asked. Gideon thought, not for the first time, that Greek gods do actually exist here on Earth.

He thought of nothing but Vangelis's detective work over the next few hours. But would it be foolish to try and track Xanthe down? What if he ended up disappointed and his memories were destroyed?

They had supper that evening outside in the warm night air. As they enjoyed sardines and French wine, he was persuaded to go to Thessaloniki to meet a man who was now curious to meet him.

Gideon asked Vangelis which God presides over the mystical ruins of Knossos on the island of Crete. He scratched his head and thought for a while and said; "Eileithyia, my friend." That rang a bell with Gideon, but he didn't know why.

"Well it's easy to forget as even we Greeks do, but legend has it that Eileithyia was born here. Many pregnant women from all over the world come here to find peace of mind, as she represented childbirth."

It meant something he knew, but nothing that came to the forefront of his mind. Maybe Xanthe had wanted a baby? He was now drawn to the place for reasons that were cryptic to him.

The Palace of Knossos was built by the Minoans and is

just south of modern-day Heraklion near the north coast of Crete. It is the size of more than two football fields, a term that made him think of Xanthe. The site came to prominence in the early 20th century when it was excavated and restored by a team led by the English, he was told.

Gideon was overwhelmed by the place as Knossos was Europe's oldest city and the palace was known globally. He enjoyed its unique frescoes and artwork but it was the Goddess Eileithyia that had him all fired up and his imagination all over the place. He learned that some said there were twin goddesses, one who made the birth come and one who made labour last longer.

Later, in the bar by the pool on that wonderful hill and after many a Greek beer, Vangelis said that he should meet this man on mainland Greece, otherwise his curiosity would burn away and make him bitter and sad in old age.

Gideon was only sad now when he was alone and after a bottle of wine, certain music would creep up on him and rip his heart out again.

The amazing Vangelis had convinced his cousins to meet with this person and explain why he should meet Gideon.

After taking the twenty-five hour ferry from Heraklion, Gideon found himself at the bustling port city on the Thermaic Gulf of the Aegean Sea, named after the ancient town of Therme, now Thessaloniki. He walked to a square and had a delicious breakfast of cheese and ham with a glass of cold beer. He then did a little sightseeing as he had three hours to fill before meeting with this stranger who would either re-break his heart or give him closure.

Gideon had not been to this city before and immediately fell in love with the place, perhaps because he was giddy with anticipation. Around every corner were old men seated at pavement cafés, smoking, drinking strong coffee and putting the world to rights, many clasping the ubiquitous worry beads.

At 1300 precisely he entered a small cafe to be greeted by a handsome gentleman in his late forties who introduced himself as Tomaso. He wore a crisp white shirt, smart dark-blue chinos cuffed above the ankle and relaxed blue boat shoes with white leather laces. He smelled not unpleasantly of tobacco.

He stood up and embraced Gideon with the warmest smile. They ordered coffee and Gideon listened to this wise man with starry eyes. He already felt like Gideon's good friend and when he had finished his opening sentences, he put two hands on his shoulders and very gently whispered, "My sister slipped away months after arriving here, without pain and in the family home. She is now in the Elysian fields and at peace, my friend."

Gideon could not breathe. He wanted to collapse, faint maybe, but the wave of shock kept hitting him.

Tomaso held onto Gideon's hands and gently told him how deeply he had loved his sister and of his misery when his mother had run away with her and abandoned him. This was the feeling that engulfed Gideon now. He felt abandoned. Empty. Left behind.

If she had loved Gideon so deeply, Tomaso said, then the man now standing in front of him must still be the same man of probity that she had loved beyond belief. As he held Gideon's hands, tears ran down his cheeks and he spoke with a rasp in his voice.

"Her head was held high. She brushed away many of the old Greek traditions and so she became a pariah within the community, a charge she accepted with dignity. She refused to care what they thought – she skipped and danced everywhere. Many of the elders could do nothing but admire her and changed their minds about their former views at the time of her parting."

Gideon's heart was palpitating. He had never seen this coming.

"She went to Nafplion to check on her house and then came back here to stay. She would not let the Navy or the old Greek traditions break her. Sure, she would cry, but she would never let them take her true self from her. She clung to it with a passion." Tomaso paused, and Gideon's mind whirled. "My friend" said Tomaso a heavy heart, "she died here at our family home after childbirth complications, some two months after she arrived back for good."

"No! No! Jesus Christ, no!" Gideon cried out. They stared at each other in disbelief. "But what – what about the child?"

"Beautiful boy..." Tomaso said, his head dropping in sadness

"No, not again for fuck's sake?!" Gideon shouted, interrupting him.

"There were twins," Tomaso said. Gideon's mind flew to Knossos and then to the boat around the headland of Marsalforn Bay. The way she had put his hand on her tummy... did she know she wanted to get pregnant? "Only one twin survived," Tomaso finished. Gideon was too numb to respond.

Perhaps seeing the state he was in, Tomaso invited him to stay with the family and offered him the villa in the garden. And so that is where he found himself later that day.

The villa was a small, enchanting old building, formerly a folly, and then converted as a home for a gardener during the 1930s. Now it was a summerhouse. As Gideon drifted into sleep there that afternoon, he fancied himself on the shores of the Styx.

Chapter Thirty-Three

Pathos

At around five in the evening, he was awoken by a housekeeper carrying a silver tray with a clean stubby glass and an ice-cold, green bottle of Greek beer. She asked if there was anything else she could do for him. He might be mistaken, he thought, but she seemed to say it in a rather flirty way. He didn't have any requests for her.

She asked if dinner up at the house would suit him and he didn't want to say yes, so he hesitated. She seemed to pick up on the sadness that had engulfed him and didn't press him any further. She just showed him a fridge full of green bottles, all dripping with condensation, and then she slipped away.

He showered and put on a clean white shirt that the housekeeper had left on a chair, and at around six, Tomaso appeared with a bottle of brandy and asked if he could come in. The housekeeper had clearly said something and this beautiful man understood Gideon's need to be away from the family, and yet also the need for company for a little while.

They were brought meat, feta, olives and bread and the brandy was mixed with a liqueur called Lovage. This English alcoholic cordial is rarely seen outside of the country so this seemed a really thoughtful gesture in his honour.

"French brandy?" Gideon noted.

"Yes, none of that awful Greek paint-stripping shit we usually serve," Tomaso laughed.

Tomaso with his rasping, tobacco-affected voice explained that Athene had studied in here and had thought of it as her secret place. It was the first time Gideon had heard that name.

"Athene?"

"I am so, so very sorry, my friend. My sister's little angel, your daughter, is called Athene, I'm so sorry, I did not think. How can you forgive me?"

"Of course I can forgive you…" His brain could not catch up with it. His daughter? "I have a daughter?!"

"Yes, but later my friend, later." And Gideon was grateful for the space in his head that had just been given to him.

He learned that Xanthe had been stationed in Malta for thirteen months prior to the Euryalus arrival and had flown back here on leave to be with her kin. On many occasions, she had actually stayed in this building. Importantly to Gideon, she thought of this as her home too and had come back here to have her child. She had sat right here where he was now. And so had their daughter. The evening was transforming into something heady and wonderful.

He woke really early with a pounding head and an aching erection. His first thought was to masturbate to rid him of his lust. Dazed, he sat up quickly as he could hear that someone was in the room. It was the housekeeper who was folding towels and setting up a small table for breakfast.

"Kaliméra!" he said. "What do I call you then, Ma'am?"

"Maria," she said and he was going to say something about that, but underneath a single white sheet, it was difficult to hide his state.

She stared at him for a moment. "Let me help you with that" she said, walking towards him.

"No!" he cried. She froze, looked upset. "I mean you no harm. I didn't mean to shout at you." He felt that her offer was genuine, but surely it would be disrespecting his hosts' hospitality and completely inappropriate in many other ways. She bowed her head slightly and left.

Lunch with the family was a pleasant affair. He arrived slightly angry and sad but soon felt strangely at home even though there seemed to be a dolorous atmosphere. Drinks were in abundance and Gideon was guided to an august lady in her seventies dressed in black. This was Xanthe's Aunt Agatha. She lifted her lace handkerchief to wipe away nonexistent tears on his cheek, then held out her arms to embrace him. She talked in Greek for five minutes and when she had finished, she squeezed his hand and said: *"Kalós órises spíti"* which meant, Tomaso told him, 'welcome home.'

Then in broken English she quoted Aristotle: "Beyond love is a being composed of a single soul inhabiting two bodies and I know you know that. God gave her a choice and she made the right one for her when she chose you."

Tomaso gently held her elbow and steered her away. He said they should eat, and Gideon asked him quietly, "You have to tell me – why is this so like a wake?"

Guiding him out to the patio, Tomaso lit a French cigarette, exhaled loudly and talked of Malta. He said there had been a heated meeting and Xanthe was instantly dismissed from the service. The reason given, with surprising leniency, was, "Services no longer required" by the Royal Navy. Gideon could understand this as the trimming down of the Service at that time gave them license to dismiss whoever they wanted under that blanket.

Tomaso said that she was not concerned with the stigma of being dismissed whilst pregnant. She had education, in fact, a degree behind her and her powerful Aunt Agatha for support, so her future should have been safe and bright. And of course she was in possession of a large pecuniary chest.

Tomaso at last spoke of the child who was born healthy. Xanthe in the throes of childbirth had cried hoarsely that she was to be called Athena. Had she known, Gideon wondered, that she, the mother, was going to be leaving this mortal coil? Aunt Agatha took the child in as her own and called her the derivative Athene as promised.

"This day is her birthday," Tomaso said. He held Gideon's hands and spoke of Xanthe, who had been taken away from him when their mother ran away to England to marry another man. Their mother had followed her dreams, he mused. "And although it was sad, ultimately, if you don't do it when you are young, the fire burns out." The family left in Greece were shamed and he was farmed out to a relative, but he never forgot the meaning of his name, he said, which translates as 'twin.'

Tomaso was Xanthe's twin! Gideon thought of the twins that Xanthe had borne him and could not control his breathing. He had not yet been shown a picture of his daughter. And where was she now?

Tomaso said that after Xanthe's death, the Aunt pondered over a surname for the child and read Xanthe's diary looking for clues. Gideon thoroughly approved. Aunt Agatha had respected her niece's heart and her wishes and had read her diary over and over, so clearly she knew that he was no cad. And here he was, vindicating that belief.

On the veranda after dinner, Tomaso and Gideon were sitting in big cane chairs and Tomaso was explaining that Athene was brought up by Agatha. The little girl was a real beauty, and intelligent too, he said. She wanted to become a chemist like her Uncle Tom and marry an Italian and move to that country to live. Such wonderful hope for one so young. She dreamed of making her way across Europe and then going to England to find her father before beginning her studies. Gideon's thought his heart could take no more.

A dozen folk had moved toward the crackling log fire even though it was warm for the time of year. Tomaso and Gideon joined them for a while, but the patio doors were open and later they walked back outside to look at the vista.

Cigarette to lips, Tomaso exhaled loudly. The smoke hung in the still air and vaporised before their eyes. "Athene was involved in an accident, crossing the road on a school trip to Athens," Tomaso said. "She was running back across the road after picking up an ice cream and she was hit by a scooter. Nobody's fault, just her own childish enthusiasm. But tragic. She died at the scene. She was eight years old at the time."

Gideon had to sit. He was speechless. Tomaso held him shaking in his arms for over ten minutes.

"We had the little girl cremated like her mother," he said later. Where her ashes lay at rest was not mentioned and Gideon felt that it would be inappropriate to ask at that moment. He was told that her body was transported back home and the family decided to keep quiet and grieve in the Greek way which clearly, they still were.

Gideon sat down and pondered the enormity of it all. Tomaso handed him a brandy.

"This had better not be any of that Greek shite!" Gideon managed to say.

Tomaso laughed as only a smoker could and hugged Gideon with one arm around him.

"Melpomene, my friend," he rasped, so quietly that Gideon barely heard him. And he would not have recognised the name if it hadn't been for what Tomaso's sister had said all those years before. Melpomene, the goddess of tragedy.

Tomaso said that Xanthe's diary contained her wishes: her ashes were to be flown to Malta and scattered on Gozo at a very special and specific place, which is exactly what was done by the faithful brother. He couldn't remember exactly where on the island, but from his vague recollections, Gideon could tell precisely what those instructions would have said.

At the ferry terminal as Gideon was leaving, Tomaso handed him a small parcel. He asked what it was.

"Something that you should open when your heart tells you to. You will just know when, my friend. Wisdom is indeed strength, you both knew, and still know. Your home will always be here, my friend. You must stay in touch, so goodbye for now. I know why she loved you so much and it has been good for my heart to meet you."

Gideon's goal in life now was to get back to Malta as soon as he could. But the Navy was taking on more commitments, and Gideon was kept busy. Unbelievably busy.

He later found himself in Australia at a missile testing range in Woomera and there he met the enchanting Mai Ling, an Australian Air Force analyst of Chinese origin. They had a meaningful affair. She flew to England to be with him and continue the relationship. But Gideon was downhearted, and when he told Mai the reason for his saudade, that nostalgic melancholy, she rightly walked away. This hurt him, nevertheless.

He later had a long, secret liaison with a gentle lady who was born without hearing. She was one of the most beautiful human beings he had ever met. She wanted children and when Gideon would not commit, it was she who pointed out his darkened heart. People were beginning to notice his thousand-yard stare, which appeared at parties, on holidays and worst of all in loving relationships.

Who would have thought that love would be found again off the prosaic A40 in West London, with the awesome Andrea? After it was over, Gideon still thought about her an awful lot. They had parted friends, but there was sadness in her eyes that haunted him. He knew that he had hurt her.

He knew he was asking these lovely women in his life to feel the same emotions that he felt. But this was grossly unfair and he was beginning to realise this and not for the first time.

The darkness deep inside him was not self-pity, he thought, but true pathos. He was still hurting and could not get over Xanthe.

Chapter Thirty-Four

The Israeli girls

Immersed in self-pity and partying for his loss, Gideon flew to the Balearic Islands in the summer of 1986.

He was in a bar in Playa d'en Bossa, Ibiza, drinking beer at eight in the morning and toking on a last cold one before getting ready for bed, having watched the sunrise in all its Mediterranean magnificence. Danny, his good friend, fellow traveller and drinking partner was already asleep back in their apartment, not ever wanting to drink again.

It was a lads' holiday. Sometimes a guy needs to be with a guy and drink uninterrupted. This belief of theirs drifted through Gideon's head beside that balmy, sensational beach, where he sat alone as the sun warmed up another glorious day in paradise.

Pachelbel's 'Canon in D' wafted from the sound system, now remixed by some unknown DJ with a rhythmic beat behind the dreamy tune. The result was heart-wrenchingly beautiful. A tear rolled down Gideon's cheek and he sighed beneath the totally ineffective ceiling fan as the chords and melody stirred at his saudade.

A deeply tanned, pretty, blue-eyed lady came across and sat on the stool next to his. Without speaking, she wiped the tear from his cheek. She slugged on her beer bottle and raised her eyebrows questioningly.

"Happy memories just make me sad sometimes," he said. "Take no notice of me, young lady. I'm dealing with it. Thank you for your concern. Very touching, but I'm on top of this. Truly."

"You wanna another beer?" she asked. Why wouldn't he? "My name is…"

He stopped her. "I want to guess."

"Great! And I'll call you Chesed until I know yours. It's the Hebrew for kindness because I can tell that you are kind.

Chesed means a whole bunch of things like grace and compassion or unfailing, faithful love. It's one of the ten Sephirot on the Kabbalistic Tree of Life."

"Is that so?" he said warmly.

Not knowing what the Kabbalistic tree was, he pondered before he spoke again. "I shall call you Marina, from Princess Marina, our old Duchess of Kent. She wore a green going-away outfit after her marriage to George, Duke of Kent in 1934. The particular shade became known as Marina Green. You're wearing a Marina Green bikini!"

"My, my. Very cool."

"Is it? Then there's more," he said, not feeling so tired now. "When I was a child, there was a puppet show called 'Stingray' on TV in England and it was about fighting all the bad guys under the sea. Marina was a young woman from one of these under-sea colonies, I can't remember which tribe she was, but the whole race was struck mute. Anyway, she joins the crew of the Submarine Stingray and becomes part of the team."

This fair 'Marina' was amused and he saw something change in her eyes. "Is this true?" she asked, and he said yes, of course! "Tell me more! Two more beers here, barkeep! Quick, or I'll lose this man and his story. A puppet, you say?"

"She, Marina that is, had been enslaved by evil King Titan of Titanica, but has escaped to the organisation 'WASP,' the World Aquanaut Security Patrol. In the very first episode, she becomes Troy's love interest. Troy Tempest being the main dude! You know, the hero."

She put her hand on her chest as if to say, "Oh! My!" and flicked her eyelashes.

Gideon swivelled on his stool to face her. "Over dinner one evening, Commander Shore, the head of this unit, presents Marina as the newest member of the Stingray crew. His daughter Atlanta is with him, and she is Troy's intended love interest. Atlanta now realises that she has a rival for Troy's affections." He finished on a quizzical note and raised his eyebrows.

"My God, what happens?" whispered the awestruck Marina in front of him.

"Well, it's left ambiguous throughout the series, but there is no doubt in any sane mind that Marina was his desire too. Now, do you want to know why am I telling you all this?"

"Yes! Yes, where are you going with it?"

"Well, it was the look Marina gave Troy throughout the series. She was so in love and yet she knew they could never be. I mean, it was a puppet, for goodness sake, and here I am at ten years old, fascinated by the eyes of a toy!" Gideon paused, teasing her. "Kinda like you are right now!"

She blushed, smiled and bowed her head.

Just then Marina's friend shimmied over and said "Tammy! What are you talking about? I could see that you were getting all fervid over here and I had to investigate!"

Marina laughed. "Avigail! You've ruined our game. You told him my name, agh! Listen to this. A puppet fishy, mermaidy woman falls for a handsome mini-submarine Captain whilst the Admiral's daughter who has the hots for him sees her claim has now been squished. And she was the Duchess of Kent."

Avigail laughed and said to Gideon playfully; "What! Are you still high from last night, Mr English?"

"Fuck off, Avi, this is the best chat-up line I've ever heard!" said Marina and they had to hold onto each other, they were laughing so hard.

Gideon wasn't really chatting her up. He was flattered, but it was just a fun way for him to talk to this attractive girl. The girls were still laughing and talking about the madness of loving looks from a marionette for over an hour. As it was approaching ten in the morning by now, the three of them decided they wanted cocktails. Soon, there were Tequila Sunrises in abundance and they drank them until midday. Gideon had been up for twenty-four hours by then and had to go and lie down urgently, but not before the girls asked if they could hook up later in a bar on the western side of the island.

Gideon really liked Marina (now sadly known as Tamara, her real name) and as the bar became livelier, it was getting harder to catch her eye, even though he could sense that she felt the same. Tamara would mouth '*later*' and blow him a kiss when they passed each other.

He bimbled back to the apartment and could not remember falling asleep, but he woke up early in the evening, hungry, and heard Danny in the shower.

They walked out and ate superb tapas at a bar on the way into town and then jumped into a taxi to Sant Antoni de Portmany on the western side of the island, a cool place to watch the sun go down. He was amazed at how fresh he felt considering the pounding his body had taken eight hours earlier. The vibes were alive on this island: the scenery, the food, the people, especially the sublime music. With unbroken sunshine during the day and a balmy evening, everything was perfect.

They went to a couple more bars before arriving at their meeting point. There was a pool on the veranda with potted palms placed in suitable locations, giving drinkers privacy without hiding them completely. Like the latticed cane work in hotel foyers all over the world, Gideon thought with warmth in his heart.

Danny came from the bar with two beers and said that he had eye-balled the girls, but another girl was having sex on the beach outside and a small crowd was watching – should they go and look? Gideon looked all round and could see Tammy and Avigail waving. This whole voyeur thing wasn't appealing to him.

The two went outside but Gideon left Danny to watch his show and went behind an upturned boat in a clump of trees to relieve himself before going back to the bar. When he got there, Avigail was outside on the veranda and reached out to take his hand. Before he knew it, she was leading him back towards the trees.

She was wearing a sheer cotton dress with a flower pattern, which she then hoisted up to her waist. She had no underwear on underneath, and they fucked, quickly and wildly against the overturned boat he had pissed on. Raw, animal, drunken sex.

She was responsive, and it was enjoyable for Gideon but he was furious with himself at the same time and as his anger grew, he got harder and pumped harder too. She kissed him emotionally and her eyes burned into his as he released inside her. Then she said, "If you hurt her, I will tell all!"

He held her for some moments. She hugged him tightly like a lover in the movies in a black-and-white railway station seeing someone off to war. They disengaged, he kissed her and he sat on the only tiny bit of sand in silence.

She smiled radiantly, blew him a kiss and walked away. The boys did not see her or Tamara for the rest of the evening, and no hotel details had been exchanged. Gideon thought of Mickey fucking that publican's wife in that Welsh toilet, then remembered Avi's warning. But after that he thought of nothing but beer as he and Danny immersed themselves in a cathartic sea of alcohol.

The evening turned into night, which turned into sunrise again at Playa d'en Bossa, back on the south side of the island.

Chapter Thirty-Five

Triangular harmony

Danny and Gideon were sitting in a bar when the two girls walked up to their table. They sat down, laughing and started to talk to them as though they had planned to meet. The boys were flabbergasted.

Avi avoided Gideon's eye and he couldn't stop thinking about his seminal fluid inside her. Much to his embarrassment, he wanted her again. They all talked lightly. It turned out that the girls were in the same unit of the Israeli Defence Force and were on leave together.

Tammy shuffled her chair around next to Gideon to say that she wanted, no, *needed*, to hear more about Marina and her beau.

"Later," Gideon said.

But Avi was having none of that and started whooping, "More, More, More!" And Danny and Tammy joined in.

Reluctantly, he started. "Ah! Marina then. Well, she can breathe in or out of the water and is mute like the rest of her race. Marina and Troy Tempest were modelled on two movie stars of the day. You can see the likeness if you know that." None around the table had the slightest clue who these characters were.

Gideon said that feminists these days objected to Marina being a bad example of a female because she was subordinate to men. That got them talking about gender roles. The girls said that Israeli women were becoming equal to men in the Defence Force and indeed, both these intelligent women were not only soldiers but they talked of specialist skills they specifically had and many more that some conscripted guys didn't have. And this had all started with Gideon's concern about how a puppet was viewed.

Tammy broke away from the serious talk, saying, "Tell me about that look Marina gave Troy again, Chesed!"

Gideon smiled. "They had different heads for different expressions, and I noticed that sometimes they didn't change Marina's head because 'that' expression said it all. So this is my thinking... the word 'id' is from Freudian psychology, as well as being a great Scrabble word. It's the part of your mind that is entirely unconscious but has hidden desires and needs. The puppeteers played on this look to appeal to the viewer's id. And I am a Marina kinda guy!"

Tammy looked at him with a dignified Marina *I want you* stare. She said, between sucking on her straw, "And I'm a Troy kinda gal!"

Avi seemed calm and distant and Danny dropped his head on the table in mock disbelief at Tamara's open invitation.

What Gideon did not know at that precise moment was that, like Troy Tempest in the puppet show, he had been selected too.

The days that followed with Tamara were some of the happiest days in his life at that time. She was bright and could talk about Nietzsche and any opera that wasn't too serious, and she asked endless questions and pondered many answers. She was ebullient almost all the time. She hinted at the atrocities that she had witnessed in action and said that this island holiday was her 'amnesia time.'

They were in a funky bar and Tamara was sipping on her Margarita when wafting through the sound system came Offenbach's 'Tales of Hoffman,' the Barcarolle with a Latino beat and no lyrics. Tammy stood up and just added her vocals. The bar stopped moving. Everyone was silent. It was one of those time-stopping moments that everyone would remember.

On a veranda that balmy evening, the two of them discussed the etymology of the name

"Ibiza. It came originally from the Arabic word 'Yabisah,' meaning 'Land.'" Tammy said. "It was the Spanish who added their own pronunciation." They quite liked Yabisah and indeed, that's what they called it from that moment forward.

"Tell me about Avigail," Gideon said on an impulse.

"Well, she's severe and fun too, and that can have mixed consequences. That's why we call her the Dark Angel. She's serious to the point of annoying and yet she can take out two targets and then save your life in an instant! She outranks me in our unit: she's the Section Commander. When we're off duty, we're sometimes lovers." She looked nervous revealing this.

That would explain Avi's 'don't hurt her' threat. Gideon smiled and held both Tamara's hands. She relaxed immediately.

"I wouldn't consider myself a lesbian, but I really enjoy the sex with her. I suppose I'm bisexual, but only with Avi. You have no idea how it can relieve the stress up at the Heights on long, dangerous patrols. With us, it's genuinely woman-to-woman stuff. You know, no dildoes but fingers and tongues and clitoral stimulation. Avi is one of the Epicurus followers and believes in natural and necessary desires. You mentioned him yesterday, and we were both amazed. I consider myself normal though, and I do like some men. Very especially you, Chesed!"

"Please call me Giddy, everyone does." Gideon thought about Epicurus and the state of ataraxia, or tranquillity, which he had learned about from Xanthe. He did bring him up in conversation from time, as he had done yesterday.

It was Gideon's turn to alter the course of the conversation and put all his cards on the table. "Avigail fucked me on the beach," he said. His heart thumped. Would this all be over now?

"I know," Tamara said. "It's her way of protecting me. That was the reason we left that evening. She was really excited about you and wanted you very badly. She could see I was aching for you too, so she was blackmailing you into you not hurting me. Giddy, this might be strange to you, but don't he angry. Try to understand. Avi made fierce love to me after we left you that time on the water's edge and as I gave her oral sex, I could taste you inside her. I knew it was you. Not a word passed between us and yet this was her way of telling me about you. Please, don't go!"

Of course he wasn't going to go, and he told her so. He thought he was the one who needed forgiveness, but she hugged him tightly and cried a river of tears.

Gideon was not sure what Danny did that evening, but he, Tammy and Avi spent the night in perfect, slow-motion triangular harmony. Tamara walked to the bedroom first, took off her Marina Green panties and lay on the bed and Gideon gently entered her without a word. Avigail then walked in naked, knelt over Tammy's face and started to kiss Gideon. Almost nothing was said between them as nature flowed along with their desires, perspiration and vibrations.

After the beautiful, life-enhancing experience of their climax together, Gideon sat on the chair by the bedside and picked up his beer as the girls held each other. They both cried tears of happiness and he could sense that something was happening, but he couldn't be sure what it was.

Tamara insisted that Gideon should come to Israel and Avigail, the more unemotional one, agreed. Gideon said that he would come and planned to book a flight to Tel Aviv as soon as he arrived back in England.

Chapter Thirty-Six

Love is like fishing

It would take two years and lots of communication before Gideon finally managed to fly to Tel Aviv in 1988. Avigail met him at the Airport and hugged him hard. The drive through the city was wild and Avi talked non-stop about how things were changing in this exciting place. There was a new resurgence and a fresh vibe as the Jewish people were riding high about their changing city. The word she used was *transition*. The drive to Haifa from Ben Gurion Airport was about 71 miles, so there was a lot to see.

Avigail was driving a very beaten-up Renault, all covered in dust and rattling away on the modern tarmac. The make-do-and-mend ethos was enchanting for Gideon. The city centre of Haifa was in decay and yet the suburbs were expanding and thriving. Haifa was deemed different in Israel as many Arabs and Arabic Jews coexisted there. It was a melting pot showing how two enemies could live side by side, a place of contradictions in which both peoples thrived. There was a lot of talk in academia, Avi said, a lot of writing and fighting about this unique place.

Home for the girls was a fabulous apartment block overlooking the ocean. The block was four storeys high and they lived in the wide, glass-fronted penthouse apartment. Tamara greeted Gideon so warmly that he knew he was home if he wished.

After a much-needed beer and with no fuss or histrionics, Tamara walked into another room and brought out a child of about two years old. "This is our daughter, Gideon, and I have named her Shoshana, Hanna for short. She was born in the May after we met."

Through all their communications, not once had she mentioned that she was pregnant. Gideon was shocked but calmed down quickly. It was so *them*, so Epicurean.

The little one looked like him, he thought as Tammy handed her over. Can one really tell at this age and stage? Tammy looked tired, still beautiful and in shape, but she had lost that military edge. She looked like a housewife and a mother, and she was a mother to the child that belonged to all three of them. Gideon was overwhelmed with the little girl, and with the little group the four of them made. It was breathtaking.

"We liked you already when you and Danny got off the bus in Ibiza," Tamara said. "I selected you, I approached you to wipe that tear from your face. That tune reminded you of someone special, we know."

He thought of Xanthe. "I'm pleased and deeply, deeply honoured," he said. "And so proud of you all." And that was all that was ever said on the subject.

In the two weeks that he stayed there, Gideon found it very different to anywhere else in the Middle East he and he had by that time visited the whole area except Iran.

One morning, he spent some time at Avigail's Army unit so she could show him around and the feeling he witnessed was one of honesty and hope. Everyone knew of her sexuality and all about her lover's sperm donor.

Gideon sat with Hanna in his arms one balmy evening as the girls talked about the Sephardi Jews from whom Avigail was descended. It was where she got her swarthy complexion from, Tammy said. He also learned about the Ashkenazi Jews, and their migration eastward to Slavic lands was heart-breaking to hear about. This was Shoshana's history too, and he was keen to take it all in.

The next afternoon when Avi was away for the day, Tammy and Gideon made love on the girl's bed. They both knew that it would be the last time for them.

Gideon had told her about Xanthe, and that she was the one lady who kept his heart beating, and Tammy said that she understood. That was the moment that he knew his journey to find the closure he needed was not over. His heart was not mended on any level. That tear that dropped because of Pachelbel's tune two years ago in that fantastic

177

bar was real. And the drops still came.

Astute and loving, Tamara held Gideon and said gently, "Never let your past experiences harm your future, sweetheart. Your past cannot be altered and Lord knows, we all bury things. But your future doesn't deserve the punishment you are giving it and neither do you! What do you want your epitaph to be? *Chased and desired by many but only caught once?* Love is like fishing, you English like to say... you will always think about the one that got away. Go find her, babe."

Chapter Thirty-Seven

The Shaman

Whilst on duty in the Persian Gulf in 1989, Gideon stumbled on a ladder on board ship and fell awkwardly on the raised hatch combing, tearing external and internal intercostal muscles. He had intense physiotherapy for a long time afterwards but nothing ever healed the wound, leaving him with frequent chest pain, and he was left believing that this was just the way it would be for the rest of his life.

After leaving the Navy in 1991 aged thirty-seven, he was in London having dinner with a Thai lady called Sanoh. When they had first met, Gideon had told her immediately of the state of his heart. Happy though he was, love was not an option for him. That avenue was now closed. Sanoh was an absolute delight to be with and understood, which is why they were such good friends. Lovers too, but extremely good friends.

He winced during the meal from his old chest pain and Sanoh said that nothing would be more efficient to relieve it than having a Thai massage. "But it must be a very particular treatment from a super-sensory Shaman who could also help the predicament of your heart," she said.

After a copious amount of champagne, he pressed her for more information. She said that her aunt in Bangkok, called Ngam-chit meaning 'good heart,' would definitely know where a 'Magic Lady' could be found to help him.

Gideon found himself in Bangkok with a former shipmate called Martin. Gideon had reconnected with this fabulous but ultimately unhappy guy at a reunion of naval personnel. They had not seen each other since training but it felt as if this was only yesterday and Gideon suggested Martin accompany him to Bangkok because he desperately needed to go there to find someone specific.

Two days into the trip, they were about to arrive at Sanoh's aunt's bar, *Madame Wann's,* which was a disco bar and cat-house. As the rain cascaded down suddenly, as it only can in Thailand, they ran the last four hundred yards to find Sanoh's relative. Sanoh had said back in England that 'Wann' was a common name in Asia and means 'sweet.' It was an omen Gideon thought, in his movie-addled, beer-fuelled brain.

They were soaked and squiffy when they ran into the bar and ordered two much-needed Singha beers from an attractive transgender bar-keep. Martin fancied the bar-keep to an extent that frankly, had Gideon curious. He asked for Ngam-chit, but it came out of his mouth, "I'm shit!" and they both fell about laughing. Rude and ignorant they knew, but this made them laugh even more because of their child-like state, and they meant no disrespect.

The bar-keep was getting annoyed with them and started muttering a string of abuse. An old lady who they had not noticed before was sitting at a rickety table against a wall drinking some sticky liquor, and she clapped her hands to stop all the tomfoolery. To their astonishment, the whole bar went silent. She beckoned Gideon over and invited him to sit down.

The background noise started again immediately and another beer was placed in front of Gideon as he quickly apologised to her. He said that Sanoh had recommended he meet with her aunt called Ngam-chit and that he was told that her name means, 'Good heart.' Her demeanour changed instantly and it was clear that he had found the long-lost aunt.

"You sleep with Sanoh," she said through knowing laughter. She gave him a toothless smile and it seemed that had cracked the code to her heart.

"Well, I have had the pleasure of waking up next to her on many an occasion. I hope you approve?"

He said that he had suffered a sports injury that had not healed, as there was no point it involving hatches, ladders and frigates in stormy seas. She said she would arrange something for tomorrow and gave him a garish business card with a golden lion on it.

Gideon later had rough sex with a girl from the bar, which seemed to him to have been a joyful experience for both of them, but he felt awful the next morning, so was gentle and passionate this time. He paid her again and she asked him to 'keep her' for the time he was there, but he was on a mission. He went back to his hotel for a shower and some breakfast and spent the rest of the morning reading in the splendid gardens and slept most of the afternoon.

At six in the evening, after a scary ride through the city in a taxi heading east and then south around the bay, Gideon found himself being driven to a district called Pattaya, sixty-two miles away. It was a party town and not what he had expected.

The very well-presented driver told him of petty crime in the beach area because of the tourists, but said that generally the place was a more mature person's choice of venue, and relatively safe.

They had arrived at what looked like a tattoo parlour with lots of dragons and lions stencilled on the window and there was no indication of the business on the other side of the glass. Gideon wasn't entirely comfortable with this at first. He believed that he could handle himself and still felt that he was invincible, which was stupid and dangerous as travel had taught him not to be in a situation like this, and yet here he was, not following his own code.

However, he paid and let the taxi leave. A neon red and gold lion was flickering, matching the image on the card in his hand, so at least he was in the right place.

Sanoh's aunt had said the lady he needed was called Madee, which means 'good start.' So there was another omen for him. He entered the place through a green door and a small bell tinkled, then he waited at the reception desk. He was pleasantly surprised at the décor and what hit him was the overwhelming cleanliness of the place. Fluffy white towels were rolled up and stacked like logs in their own little pigeonholes and beautiful ethereal music soothed him. The instrument playing was a lute with four strings called a *Pipa,* a Chinese instrument, he had been told.

After some uncomfortable minutes, the much-awaited Madee appeared looking like a painting of a faded dignitary etched on a Ming vase. She was very beautiful but aloof and dignified too. Gideon showed her the card and she was expecting him, so no introductions were exchanged.

She had a kind of majestic grandeur. She looked in her early sixties and was wearing an *áo dài* which was jet black with a high collar, and white trousers. Her hair was piled high, skewered with bits of bamboo and decorated with red lotus blossoms. He had learned that different colours of this flower take on different spiritual meanings. Red signifies enlightenment, ascension or rebirth.

This matriarch was cold and unsmiling at first as he paid the amount of money agreed back in Bangkok.

Her age intrigued him, although who would not be proud to have someone who looked like that on his arm anywhere in the world, he thought? She was certainly many years his senior. He liked her immediately despite her world-weary expression, which suggested a distrust of all things western. She beckoned him through to the back of the building and for the hundredth time in his life, he found himself on the set of a Charlie Chan movie.

She sat him down on a plain wooden chair and although she was speaking in her native tongue, her tone appeared to be full of sympathy. After giving Gideon a cold beer, which he downed in one go as he was nervous, she asked him to take his footwear and clothes off, save the underwear. She then gestured for him to lie down on a kind of inspection futon and touched him gently all over, including parts of his body that he thought at that moment were not relevant, such as his temples, ankles and inner thigh. The thigh part was erotic, make no mistake he thought and he tried to relax.

It was, undeniably, part of the mystical examination. Madee sighed heavily and said, "My name is Madee," in a frustrated but kind way. Then she whispered, "Please relax!"

His spirits lifted as she had passed her hands over his intercostal area, which magically warmed up when touched, the heat going deep into the muscle. He had not mentioned where his injury was at any stage. She had just found it.

After about ten minutes of this, she led him to another room which frankly, Gideon thought, looked like a brothel, albeit a clean, modern version with incense sticks burning and candles lit. All natural light was shut out and there was only a big square table at knee height with a soft covering. As she left the room briefly, he was disappointed. This was not what he had come for and he did not want to be paying for sex again!

After some minutes she came back in dressed like an exotic dancer in a short silk kimono-style gown tied at one side of the waist with a silk cord and matching shorts which were pleasing to the eye. He admired the tattoo on her left leg that had a tail poking out and disappeared up and under her garment. She watched his face and could surely see his startled look and that he could not take his eyes off the tattoo.

Remaining dignified and now with a certain power over him, she slowly untied the silk cord and slipped the kimono off her shoulders. She held this position for a moment before letting it fall to the floor. She slipped out of her brief shorts so that he could see her artwork in full and it was a formidable and glorious serpent. She turned around to show him the full effect. The serpent's tail fattened on her thigh then went up and over her hip and up the left side of her torso, then down to the majestic head in line with her umbilicus. There were yellow, pink and blue flowers around the reptile with some luscious green foliage in between and its angry mouth had fangs poised to strike. It was a magnificent work of art, and so was she.

Chapter Thirty-Eight

The white lotus flower

It was dim in the room but Gideon could see that she was extraordinarily beautiful. He liked small breasts, and Madee had almost none to speak of, which made her even more desirable. Her skin was that of a thirty-year-old with only the faint beginnings of crow's feet to show the world her age. The tiny wisp of soft black pubic hair added to her mystique.

Madee flipped the kimono back up over her shoulders and without putting back on her shorts, secured the cord in a knot as she motioned to him to lie on his back. She made hand signs to take his underwear off too and passed him a towel to cover his private parts. His penis was not erect, but fattened a little and grew longer as thoughts of this mystical person set his libido on fire.

She sat in the Lotus position by his feet and gently lifted his right foot, resting it on her soft pudenda. If she had asked if he wanted a relief massage at that stage, he would have capitulated no matter what the cost.

The guzheng music now playing began to set off a Pavlovian response, reminding him of his Australian lover as Madee massaged his foot and ankle so deeply and expertly that she had total control over his whole relaxed being, including his brain.

Gideon wondered why she started the treatment at his feet although he really didn't care as it was so pleasing and he was pain-free already, and she was nowhere near his chest. Since she was a Shaman, a male admiring the female body was all part of the treatment, he had been told in England. It was working well in Thailand.

Madee moved all over Gideon, never breaking the connection of her touch. Even when she had to get up to walk around him to change position, she was constantly in contact with his body.

She asked at one stage if he was OK as she was behind him with her legs and arms wrapped around like a koala on a gum tree.

Gideon was for some reason losing his voice, but in the most meaningful way he could croak, he said, "Just hold me, please." She did this for some minutes and then started to move her hands all around him again and to pull and stretch his limbs.

Xanthe had been right. He has always been sentient and this serpent was tapping into that sensory conduit and had him incapable of ever moving again if she so wished. Her piped music was ethereal and haunting and it was hard for him sometimes to contain himself when individual notes hit his personal 'G-spot' while engaged in this physical contact. Would it have been the same experience without the music? Of course not, it was part of the treatment.

"Your heart hurts more than your body!" she said suddenly. "Let me take you somewhere only I take you, please?"

Slender, almost skeletal, she had a softness of skin that was unctuous and the appearance and touch of a butterfly. He had not wanted to embrace someone so desperately since Malta, which was not going to happen, he knew. When she said 'take you somewhere…' she meant in the mind and the heart. However, Gideon's thoughts were most definitely salacious.

After the hour was up, Madee looked at him like a mother concerned about her child's health. She told him that if he was to take this seriously then he should come back and see her tomorrow.

He sat up and stroked the area in front of her ear with his thumb and managed to reply, "Yes please, if I may?"

"You must take this seriously," she said. Goodness, he wanted to hug her, but he picked up one porcelain hand and kissed the back of it as they made the date.

Getting a taxi back to Bangkok was easy with Madee's help and blessing. It was like having his own chauffeur, such was her power and respect. He could hardly speak, he thought with a strange new happiness.

The rain still lashed down on all the tin roofs as they drove through the shanty-town of folklore as they now approached Bangkok once more. A sad song wafted mournfully from the radio.

Back at Madame Wann's bar, Gideon's buddy and the bar-keep had gone off somewhere and he was never to see Martin again. And Ngam-chit never saw her employee again either. Far from being angry or mystified, Gideon wished them both well, as did the toothless aunt, although she was cross at losing a good worker.

Gideon called the aunt 'Melissa' after the Greek goddess of bees and honey. Honey is sweet and it also means 'pleasant sounding' in Greek which is what her niece's name, Sanoh, means in Thai. She didn't understand really, but he found Ngam-chit hard to pronounce so it was Melissa from now on. She didn't seem to mind, and they became good friends.

The next day Gideon arrived back at Madee's. She sat him down with a cold beer. "Beer good! Nam keng." She put her eerie music on and looked him in the eye. "What I will give you will be relief from your chronic pain. I will relax the sympathetic nervous system."

Gideon was now lost and attentive beyond belief. She talked about 'feed and breed' and 'rest and digest.' He had little idea of what she meant but understood her earnest delivery, and that she now cared about him.

In the parlour, a young girl of about sixteen silently drifted in and motioned for him to put his feet in an ornate bowl full of warm water. He did, and the girl washed his feet.

After he lay down, rather than rubbing and kneading as in other types of massage, Madee started 'lengthening' those stretches again as though she was gently trying to pull his leg off. She used rocking motions to support his flexibility, enhance his circulation, and ultimately relieve his years-old pain.

"I will help your joint and flexibility to give you an inner calm. No effleurage!" she said with a tone he had not heard before from her. In addition to the stretches, she also incorporated compression and acupressure.

Madee said gently, "My method will increase your circulation, infuse your tissues with nutrients and oxygen. It will disperse carbon dioxide toxins and this will help your body be more efficient so it won't get old too soon."

Who could argue, looking at this beautifully aged, delicate doll? After an hour, she quietly backed off and sat down by his feet. Gideon couldn't move. It was the perfect moment and he had not such peace since Marsalforn all those years ago.

"Ataraxia," he said, with love in his heart.

Madee didn't bring him another beer and he did not protest. He couldn't drink even if he wanted to. He understood who was in charge. As he lay there, he thought that he had not paid her up front this time. His brain was the only thing working in his collapsed and relaxed state.

After another hour or so, he had no idea of time anymore, she arose from her chair and beckoned him to follow her up the stairs. At the top there was an incredible fortress of an entrance that was opened with an old-fashioned safe dial.

Once inside, the most exotic, clean, minimalistic, enchanting apartment lay before him. She stood by the door and held one arm out as if to say 'come this way if it pleases you,' without actually saying a word.

He wanted to say something like "Are you sure?" but that would have been so bloody western, and anyway he was struggling to speak at all, so he walked in. Gideon was invited to stay with her for the rest of his visit. He was carrying his backpack, which was his only luggage, and so he stayed.

The silence in that apartment was wonderful considering the city that surrounded it. She didn't say anything later that evening until he entered her, and then she let out a wondrous gasp, followed by a gentle passage of Thai as she held him tightly and ran her fingers through his hair.

Gideon was to learn over the next two weeks that the practice of Thai massage is thousands of years old and it is still part of Thailand's medical system due to its perceived healing properties. This is at both emotional and physical levels, and he liked this very much. He told Madee of his saudade. He told her that that he believed Aeolus spoke to him.

English culture sometimes accepts shamanic healing practices such as the increasing intensity of massage Madee performed in the four further sessions he had with her. He loved the crossover of cultures. She explained the concept of the more conservative of the two major traditions of Buddhism, the *Theravada Metta* which means loving and kindness and is based on the 'Doctrine of the elders,' an integral part of her practice.

There was Greek in there too! Madee said over dinner one evening, "Plato wrote that astral mysticism in the classical world reflects the human psyche and is composed of the same material, therefore explaining the influence of the stars upon human affairs." This took Gideon by surprise, but what she said next made his heart weep.

"Search out that ethereal element in that plane which is inhabited by an Angel. Go kiss that wind."

Madee's procedure and rhythm of massage was adjusted to fit the receiver. This included everything she did. Sometimes they would eat without speaking. Her actions were as erotic as they were healing and she was changing him in front of her. She knew precisely what she was doing and every time he went to say something dumb, she would put her chopsticks across her delicate mouth and frown. How did she know? How could she tell?

Gosh, how he loved all this playing and teasing and importantly, learning. He noticed that he had been given a spoon and fork for the meal simply because using two sticks to eat with caused him anguish. He would bring her thoughts, feelings and calm back to England.

The last time Gideon saw her was as he tried to get into his taxi to leave. She held him back and hugged him so hard that he was surprised that such a delicate frame could exert such pressure. She looked up at Gideon and he saw a tear on each cheek and she wore the white lotus flower in her hair. At the time, he had no idea that this signifies the "victory of the awakened mind." She, on the other hand, would have known this and Gideon would weep at her symbolic gesture for the rest of his life. Victory indeed.

She had re-awakened Gideon and altered his way of thinking. She had shown him that although nobody could take Xanthe's place, someone could step in.

Chapter Thirty-Nine

The lawyer

Gideon had embarked on a career in the hospitality trade after leaving the armed forces in 1991. Three years later, at forty years old, he found himself the Area Manager of a string of licensed properties on the South West coast of England.

He was told to meet a lawyer from his employer. There had been a tussle in the bar that he managed when a thoroughly unpleasant person refused to leave after closing time was called. In the ensuing mêlée, they had tripped as Gideon struggled to relieve him of his makeshift weapon and their combined weight had them crashing into a pool table with the offender's skull as the buffer, which was regrettable, but for Gideon, unavoidable.

Gideon had to go to London to be seen by a particular company lawyer in some seedy office in bustling Victoria. The person on reception was clearly Bengali as a small green flag with a slightly offset red circle towards the hoist was pinned to her shirt. She buzzed her superior and then walked him into a surprisingly sumptuous, albeit cluttered office.

Having been interrogated by military experts, he knew how to hold his own in a situation like this. The woman lawyer was dressed in a tailored pinstriped power-suit with expensive heels, and it was easy for him to stay focused on her dark eyes. She shook his hand and he didn't take his gaze away for a second. To Gideon, who's mood was angry, this seemed to spook her a little and she gestured to a chair the other side of her desk as she sat down.

"My name is Anushka Patel and I require a brief synopsis of the truth or as near to it as possible, please," she said in an almost dismissive, but authoritative tone.

This opening salvo he liked, though. To him, it meant

that she did not want any whimpering excuses. Intelligent and with a no-nonsense approach, she was showing that although he was innocent until proven guilty, she knew that a potentially violent man was sitting just across her desk.

Gideon spoke quietly and with confidence, "A known alcoholic ne'er-do-well, who was extraordinarily drunk and refusing to leave the premises, as he thinks the law doesn't apply to him, had to have his drink taken from the bar and poured down the sink. Tired of his asinine stupidity, I walked around the said bar and onward to the exterior door to unlock it for him to leave. The moron, for truly, he is a moron, walked toward the exit, and unbeknown to me, picked up a pool cue and in one action, had the weighty, leaded end swinging towards my unprotected head. This would undoubtedly have left me with life-changing injuries had I not responded so quickly!"

The lawyer swivelled in her chair whilst playing with her lips with her pencil. "It says here that your response was excessive and uncalled for," she said, like a police interrogator.

"I have read that too," he said. "It's an assumption and not a fact. Suppose one suddenly stabs a pencil into the back of an unsuspecting person's hand in a library or a church? In that case, their sudden outburst of profanities is natural. It can't be controlled and it can't be helped."

She hummed and nodded. She couldn't disagree.

"I naturally and immediately defended myself and during that mêlée, the force of my forward motion had him falling backwards and as we tumbled, his head hit the side of the pool table. The irony of that, eh?" he said, without emotion in his voice.

"How do you account for the injuries to his face?" she said.

"Unexplainable in the heat of battle, Ma'am!" he said, actually believing this.

She thought for a minute, made some notes, swivelled around and said, "Any regrets?"

"All injuries are regrettable in conflicts, Ma'am."

"That's not what I asked!" she snapped back at him.

Just then a male colleague walked in unannounced, put some papers on her desk and said; "These need your eyes, Annie." He then walked away without acknowledging Gideon.

She spat out, "I despise men who think they can just walk in here and bark an order as though I'm of no consequence!" She genuinely seemed upset and Gideon thought he would be too. She bit her bottom lip, exhaled and said to the room; "My name is Anushka, not Annie." And then to Gideon, "I loathe the English way of being what they perceive as pally!"

"Misogynist prick, is he?" he said, and she smiled. He said without further invitation; "So you are an Indo-Aryan ethnolinguistic person native to South Asia who dislikes being labelled an Indian?"

"Not so," she said. So that put him back into his smart-arsed place!

"At school, I was called many horrible things and I came to realise that it was deemed normal, and generally it was not meant as a racist remark. With some, it was, for sure, and yet in my area of London, others used it as though they thought it was almost a term of endearment. Where are you staying tonight?" She caught him off balance with the question.

"A boutique hotel on the Bayswater Road. It will suffice until I can jump on any train heading south tomorrow."

"Bayswater, Bayswater…" She turned this over in her thoughts and then gave him a business card and said, "Meet me here at eight this evening. I'll have all this sewn up and you can sign it and leave the rest to me. And don't eat first as the meal is on my expenses."

Gideon stood up and shook her firm hand. He looked at the card and it said, "The Ganges… authentic Bangladeshi food." The restaurant was nowhere near the Bayswater Road.

"Shouldn't that read The Padma Naadī?" he said. "We learned about this at HMS Ganges, you know, the etymology, and I believe as the Ganges flows through your country, you guys change the name?" He didn't give her time to think and went on, "I love all Indian food, but food from a river in Bangladesh? A trifle risky, methinks?" He was gently trying to provoke a reaction.

"A stereotypical and racist thought, Sir. Let a proper 'Indian' show you how wrong you can be. And you should know that I am a Bengali from Bangladesh. Bengali is an ethnicity and Bangladeshi is a nationality."

Gideon had had no idea.

"What's your favourite colour?" she said.

"Why would you ask?"

"You write with a green pen. It's unusual; it must mean something to you. So colour is important in your life?"

"An astute observation. I've always had a thing about women in white."

He had only been with her for ten minutes and she had him all worked out. She looked vaguely familiar, too.

Anushka was there drinking wine when he arrived at the restaurant. She was wearing the tightest white dress he had ever seen, apparently sprayed on by a painter. Black heels matched her clutch bag. He thought this was a power thing, but soon began to change his mind.

They sat down and she smiled as she poured another glass of wine for herself and raised her full eyebrows to ask gently if he would like some too? He would, but asked for a beer first. The menu came and he could see no Bengali beer and being in the licensed trade, he knew that some of the best Indian beer was brewed in England these days. To his surprise, there was Chinese *Tsing Tao* beer which, as it's made from rice, would be the perfect starter for this meal.

"I have ordered for you as you said you had never been to my parents' country of birth. I assume that will be okay?" Of course it was. This had become a pattern in his life and one he liked very much indeed. Powerful females were asserting themselves.

"To business first. Sign here, here and here and forget about everything. I have contacted the right people and this incident will now be closed. Ask me no more. This perpetrator is known to the police and self-defence is accepted. Just! On the darker side, he has many strong connections in the soccer hooligan community and they do not forgive easily."

Gideon wasn't concerned, but he liked the caring attitude.

"Talking of football, you and I have met briefly before when you were at Wembley Stadium as a guest. After that, I had to make it my business to find out everything about you so that I could vet you for the post that you now hold. I was involved in the purchase of the five properties in Devon. I was in acquisitions at the time."

Gideon remembered the drink supplier's invitation to Wembley to see an international football game, but did he remember her? He had a vague memory of her standing next to him in a PR photo. He was not one to make a move on a woman, but how silly of him not to have noticed her back then!

It turned out that she had been in Devon when the company took those five units in sleepy Ilfracombe, with that misogynist from her office. At that time, Gideon had far too much to oversee already and another five business units with all their individual headaches played heavily on his mind. He had not focused on the individual 'suits' who were circling that day.

"Goodness me, you look… good enough to eat!" he said now. He had been thinking 'esculent.'

"Hey! Let us eat first. Bad boy!" she said, and then went on, unabashed, "We often skip what the English deem a traditional starter and have this instead." It was an aromatic course made from bitter vegetables and herbs, steamed and served with small cubed potatoes. "It's called Shukto and it's offered in tiny portions." With spoons, they dipped into rice and then the vegetables and the bitterness was a real surprise.

The taste was fabulous, but he had wanted to continue his charm offensive as she didn't seem to have taken offence.

"You really are alluring."

"How charming and kind of you. Now, eat. My family say this is of great medicinal value. The main ingredient used in today's dish is kôrola, which is a form of bitter gourd.

The number of ways to prepare this dish is mind-boggling, depending on the region one comes from. It is a very complex dish and traditionally, it is a critical measure of a Bengali cook's abilities in the kitchen. Today, for you, there is shrimp in it too. So it's now a critical measure of how you perceive me."

Gideon was impressed. She had him embarrassingly hooked. Play hard to get, Gids, he told himself. Hard. He leant forward, arms on the table. "How unbelievably thoughtful. I assume that you are trying to seduce me, and if that's the case, I am going to state that my resistance has just gone over the hill with its arse on fire."

"Call me Anushka, please?" she said. "I simply love that chain around your neck. So unusual."

Chapter Forty

We?

"Which region are you from then, Anushka?"

"I was born in Tower Hamlets here in London, so I'm a 'Steak and chips' girl. But I also like a shrimp cocktail, which they do really rather well in many Indian restaurants, and I say with pride! And yes, I'm a Hindu, but I eat beef. Surprised?"

He was surprised, but not in the way she thought. He had come to London to get himself out of a complicated legal situation and within the day, he had eaten bitter gourd, been cleared of any wrongdoing and now it would seem, the Hindu goddess Parvati was about to seduce him.

She slept with Gideon in his trendy boutique room that night. In the morning after making love again, Anushka said, "I speak a little Hindi too, and although it's good to argue with my mother from time to time, I consider myself English now and I am losing the native language, a situation that I am comfortable with!"

"I have no right to pry, but I see that you're married?"

"Yes. But he converted to Islam. People have been coming over here from Bangladesh since the war, but when a new wave came in the seventies, preachers really had a grip on the new communities. All the English probably noticed was that Bangladeshi restaurants suddenly stopped selling alcohol. It was because of the imams."

Gideon nodded. She seemed to him an assimilated, vibrant and wonderfully talented person who was living her dream, and a part of her background culture was trying to drag her back two thousand years.

"But temperance was a step too far for some curry houses. Some of them found a theological loophole that allowed non-believers to bring their own alcohol. There was a real tension in the community over this issue. My husband no longer drank because of his newfound faith. Everything changed between us almost overnight."

The following Friday, they were both in a rented chalet in the most serene part of Devon, behaving as though they had known each other forever.

Gideon had driven down to the coast and Anushka's vehicle was already there. He ran up to the veranda, swung through the double doors and stopped dead in his tracks at the sight that greeted him.

It was the bindi on her forehead that meant everything to him. Yes, he knew it symbolised that the woman is married but it could also mean other things. She was indeed still married but she said she was wearing it as a 'third eye' as she wanted to ward off bad luck. It was a large vermillion dot and she had unique white swirls painted like waves over her eyebrows. She was also wearing a substantial white blouson tied at the waist with nothing else on except for deep-red lacy panties.

The transition for Anushka and Gideon now accelerated to the speed of light as she had handled Gideon's case so well that she received promotion and was able to leave her overbearing husband and move to the West country. There was no moral dilemma for her.

Gideon was talking one evening about the freedom to pray to whoever one wants. This was fine with him in England, but in a marriage where two different traditions are opposed, it can be such a problem, and indeed, Anushka's struggle had been immense.

Over the meal that evening, Anushka said, "Bangladeshis live in a small piece of land where they are never exposed to a diverse multi-ethnic culture. Many of the Bengalis in India fled to escape from the Pakistani army in 1971. It's pretty fucked up!"

"Look at the United Kingdom," Gideon said. "Look how divided with distrustful we can be. Celts versus Saxons, the North despising the South, Cornwall thinking it's a different country, everyone hating the English! Christ, then there's the Welsh! But I love the Welsh!"

"And I love you, Gideon, and I am never going to leave you." They had been together for over a year.

He had changed with the wonderment she had brought to his darkened heart. As he held and hugged her, kissed her brow and then her nose, he whispered; "I will never leave either, I promise, I promise."

She introduced Gideon to Tantric sex. It was slower than regular sex and involved copious amounts of alcohol. He had been around the world three times and here in Devon was the gateway to a Bangladeshi heaven.

They flew to Rhodes on a snap, last-minute flight, which cost almost nothing. Gideon knew the place well enough to show her this amazing part of the Greek islands away from the masses.

Prasonisi was a small islet that during low tide showed an isthmus so, depending on the weather, one could walk to the southern tip of Rhodes Island. Not many people visited the beach at that time as there was not much in the way of facilities.

When the tide was out, he told her, you could stand with one leg in the Mediterranean and the other in the Aegean. Anushka did just that. She looked Gideon straight in the eye and said, "Nobody can get really close to you, Giddy. As much as I love you, it's a Sisyphean task for me just trying. Enjoy her memory, but don't let her become an emotional albatross around your neck. Unless that's actually what you want? She is preventing us from being what you and I should be by now!"

She then said, "I've chosen, *premee*. Now you choose which sea you need to be in."

Premee was Hindi for 'lover' and she didn't need to say which 'sea' she had chosen, because she'd had the courage of her convictions when she changed her life for him. She was now pleading with Gideon's heart to do the same! She was right to do this because it put him in a position he could not evade.

Aeolus, the Greek keeper of the wind, gently blew her hair and the short, wraparound sari she was wearing, which billowed as she said through her tears, "Is that her in the wind Gideon, you bastard? If she comes with you, then I'll take her on too. I want you that desperately!"

Gideon thought of the Greek philosopher Epictetus and his phrase; *'It's not what happens to you, but how you react to it that matters.'* Happiness is indeed how one reacts and Anushka-the-Brilliant knew this too.

"Let's get married. I mean it," he said. "No, truly, I mean it!"

Many weeks later in a cosy, trendy hotel in Cornwall and under the fluffiest duvet in the world, she started giggling and when Gideon asked her what she was happy about she said, "I came off the pill before our last trip, my love."

He rolled her over on her back and kissed her pubic hair lightly and then kissed it all the way to her umbilicus and then laid his head on that flat, deep-brown, warm stomach and shed a tear. She stroked his hair and wept a little too.

On the Monday morning, they parted for fourteen days. Much later in the day, she called him from her head office in London and said her favourite Aunt had invited her to the wedding of her nephew. Was it okay with Gideon if she went? Of course, he couldn't be happier for her. Some days later she said that she had tickets for her and her mother to fly to Shahjalal International Airport.

Gideon had assumed the wedding would be in Brick Lane, or maybe as far away as Birmingham. But Dhaka, in Bangladesh? He really had not thought of that. He missed her so badly already and she hadn't even left yet. He had never had a jealous moment, but he felt a pang that he had not had before. Still, he knew she was savvy enough to handle her disjointed family. He went to London the night before she was due to fly out.

They made love like teenagers in the morning and then just held each other until it was time for her to depart. He took his chain off, the one she admired so much, and put it around her neck. She said that she didn't want to go without him, which was deeply touching, and he believed her.

They were standing in the rain in Victoria and she put

199

his hand on her tummy and whispered, "We love you so much, Gideon. Always and forever." A Biblical downpour mingled with her sobbing. His gifted chain seemed to glisten in the drabness of that bleak London day against her beautiful dark skin.

Chapter Forty-One

The Abyss

Anushka went to pick up her mother and then on to London Heathrow.

Gideon sat in a pub at Paddington Station. He ordered two pints to save him going back up to the bar and began to neck them as though they were his last.

He knew which aunt she had meant now. Her mother's sister was always chatting on the phone to her from Bangladesh. She was seen as a westernised woman who was 'stuck' back home and she was the mother Anushka never had and always really wanted.

It was all good. She knew what she was doing. He just missed her so very much. Two more beers please? Yes, of course. Anushka was incredibly good-looking, bright and interesting to be around and had a surprising rapier-like wit, always pointing out some idiosyncrasy in someone they knew for them both to laugh at. And yet he had a terrible feeling in his gut for absolutely no reason. Was it something to do with her shifty husband? Why he had been so quiet lately?

His painful instinct came to fruition. He never saw Anushka again.

After the two-week period she was supposed to be away, he received no call. He wasn't too worried, but he was gut-achingly empty. He risked a call to her parents' house and there was no answer. He left it for another week and then called her office.

"Yes, awfully strange that? Annie has not contacted us either," said her paper-throwing colleague. Gideon wanted to scream at him that her name was Anushka, but he needed him on his side.

Frustration, anger, sadness and confusion now overwhelmed him, but he had businesses to run and people depending on him and life has to be kept going.

After some six weeks of hearing nothing, he went to the police. They could do nothing as she had willingly gone abroad and so he went to the Bangladeshi High Commission in Kensington. His persistence paid off and he was eventually assigned a 'controller.' At least it was someone to talk to. He was kind and sympathetic, but Gideon soon realised that luring people back to their country of origin was very common, especially children and wives who 'went astray!'

Terrible things went through his head as he now knew he would never know of her fate. His heart went dark as he thought of her miles away in some mountain village, perhaps chained up, perhaps raped, perhaps used to breed six children.

He went to her parents' house not far from Brick Lane and a 'relative' said that the whole family had moved up to Birmingham. He screamed at Gideon with hate in his eyes, "You bloody bastard English, go away!" Gideon hated such bigotry.

Gideon had no closure and never would. A year or so down the line, he called her office again and they tactfully said that she left of her own accord so there was no reason for them to get involved with his search.

"Are you not concerned?" he retorted in a raised voice.

"Not at all. Smart girl. She knew what she was doing." Then the penny dropped. Racism of the highest order.

He had to let go. He hoped that she had somehow got away. He often fantasied that his thoughts were being transmitted to her somehow. Silly, but cathartic for him. Should he go there and get her out? Not a chance. When he had had too many Chinese beers, which was often, he used to talk to a God he didn't believe in and ask if he could whisper in her ear that he was missing her, and she should never give up on him. Pathetic he knew, but essential for the soulless, and truly, he was soulless again.

When he found a break in his calendar, he went back to Devon and rented 'their' chalet again and locked himself away for ten days in a quagmire of self-pity and grief.

One hung-over morning he was trying to focus his eyes, and he saw, drawn with a marker pen on the wooden bedpost, a letter and then a figure and then another letter: 'A4G.' It was on the side of the bed she liked to sleep on and as he sat up, he realised that she must have doodled this one sleepy morning when he was in the shower or getting cups of tea. How childishly wonderful that this sensible, law-abiding adult would leave graffiti behind.

The loving scribble made Gideon think that as the rain came down on the chalet, all the available routes to find her had come up against a wall of silence. This was not the movies. His search had reached no happy ending, in fact there was no ending at all.

Did he have a child now in Bangladesh? Was she bullied because of her colour?' Somehow he imagined a girl. And wherever his lover was, he pictured her in physical and mental pain.

Gideon wept at the thought of it all.

Chapter Forty-Two

The diary

Gideon finally flew to Malta in 2002 and stayed at the Dragonara Hotel at St Julian's Bay in Sliema. He was now forty-eight years old.

As he entered the bar for the first time, an attentive waiter asked if he wanted to be seated and showed him to an alcove. He ordered a JC and said that he would be staying a week.

"My preferred sundowner is this, my beloved JC," he said, "but I also like a Tequila Sunrise." The waiter bowed and Gideon chuckled to himself. Is there an irony in having a Sunrise as a sundowner?

The first morning, Gideon made some enquiries and popped out to look at some local buildings. He had rented a dilapidated, dust-covered deuce-coup with no badges in evidence, so it was hard to know what make it was. It was not officially roadworthy, with four bald tyres and some of the wire bands visible through the worn rubber, but he loved it and was pleased that the circling bureaucrats in Europe had not totally 'won' over these extraordinary people yet.

The heart-wrenching White Mansions was now an embassy among other things, but at least the building was still in use. It still looked very English, which pleased him. He sat on the steps and wept.

Everything had changed to accommodate the mass tourism that had exploded over the years. It still had a charm though, and it warmed his heart when he overheard a sunburnt family from the Midlands of England exclaiming, "It's nothing like Bartley Green is it?" in that unique Birmingham drawl.

Gideon was appalled at the litter and the ubiquitous plastic water bottles and he despaired of all human beings at times. Then when he was having a cold beer in an ancient

1940s style bar, the charm of the place filled him with joy again and he concluded that the human race had not spoiled this entire, very special island.

Back in the Dragonara Bar later that day, Gideon noticed a smartly dressed American lady who now walked over and engaged him in conversation, gently and openly flirting with him. Her name was Jessica. She was slightly older than him and beautiful in her advanced years in a way that American money can achieve. Immaculately dressed with oyster-white teeth, she was here to research some movie locations and it seemed very natural to talk to her.

"You intrigue me!" she said, throwing her head back haughtily. Gideon bought her a drink and she said she worked out of New York and lived in Boston, Massachusetts.

The commute was around four hours on the train, she informed him, and just over an hour by air. The railway was her preferred method of transport as all the faffing around at airports made the journey tiresome. "I am a traveller, not a tourist, and sometimes I'm just a damn commuter!" she said and he loved her ballsy attitude.

"I don't want to know about you and why you're here just yet…" she teased, "I need to work this one out myself. This is what makes you intriguing to me. I'm leaning towards history?"

"Very much so," Gideon said.

She drank Bourbon on the rocks and he thought how stereotypical-American and perfectly lovely that was.

She was a freelance scout contracted to a firm that scrutinised places for film locations. Being self-employed meant she got to call the shots. "I get handed a script that has already received the go-ahead, and as soon as my company receives the money, I break the seal and read that script, and then I'm given a blank cheque to fly anywhere in the world. The internet makes my life much easier, but much less exciting!"

"I want your job!" Gideon said.

"Certain scenes will be highlighted with suggestions

written next to them, but sometimes not, which I much prefer. Then off I go! I have to get the entire movie in my head many times and sometimes I need to find the soul of a particular scene to envisage the perfect location."

The eyes of Jessica the Bostonian betrayed her seductive thoughts. He leaned forward and touched her cheek and said that his heart was elsewhere right now and he had to be alone until Aeolus helped him to find the closure that he had come here to seek.

He explained about Aeolus over a delicious dinner of Barbounia. She dabbed the corner of her mouth with an immaculate white serviette and asked him to inform reception when Aeolus had helped, and to let her know when, and if, he did end his chapter. Gideon bowed his head slightly and said that he would.

The next day he took a modern air-conditioned bus to the ferry crossing at Cirkewwa as he hoped it would still take him the long way around and through streets one would never find with only a tourist map. He missed the rickety, crucifix-bedecked old Bedfords that used to run up to here. This bus didn't take the long way round.

The twenty-five-minute crossing to Gozo was so lonely and all he could think about was those aubergine-coloured lips and her aroma.

He hired a quad bike, which was practical and convenient and yet paradoxically it upset him that this small island had succumbed to such modernity. He biked to a magical place to them which was near the ruins of Sopu Tower on the eastern side of the island.

He did not have the courage at first to walk down that goat track to 'their bay' in case he came across deckchairs and the beach covered in litter, then memories would have been partly distorted. But to end it by the tower would be craven. She would have loved him thinking of that word! And indeed, he thought with a newfound sedate belief, he was about to walk down to her resting place.

So then he walked down to their beach where her ashes were let free to dance with Aeolus forever.

There was never anyone around that bay with its red sand in 1971 and there was nobody there today, perhaps because Aeolus knew he was coming. Gideon's heart had told him to open the parcel on that beach, the one Tomaso had given him on the dockside at Thessaloniki. As the wind blew around him, he tore off the paper and found Xanthe's diary for 1971/72, as he had almost guessed he would. As he slowly read page after page and took in what they said, he had the urge to tear those paper sheets out one by one, and let Aeolus give her history back to her. But he read avidly on.

On the page dated Saturday, August 14th 1971 she had written:

"I felt something different for the first time. It was a boy. My first boy and verily, he was a beautiful boy. I've seen him twice in one week since the Euryalus berthed at St Angelo and there seems to be a way about him that I can't fathom. Why has it affected me so?

At the Communication Centre yesterday, he was in a small working party to identify sensitive equipment. There was the limaceous Nigel, who frankly, is an anachronism from the Victorian era and his uncouth, hilarious Leading Seaman (Mickey I think?) and then my boy. He had a cool head and had deep judgement in his eyes and clearly adored his barbarian leader and abhorred the capricious Nigel. Oh dear. His stare overpowered me as he turned to look at me for the first time and inexplicably, he was the most commanding person in the foyer. I simply have to see him again! Thank goodness for my knowledge of Red Indians. I must look into it, it is giving me ideas."

Gideon flicked forward many, many pages to see what she had written when her wonderful 'Red Indian' idea had come to fruition on that very beach. Tears streamed down his face.

He turned back to the page he was on and thence to the Sunday that followed, and it read, "It was easy to arrange a visit to the Operation Room yesterday on the Euryalus for my girls. Lord knows, those sailors were falling over themselves to accommodate our needs and yet all I had on my mind was that boy."

What struck Gideon was that there was no "What am I doing?" or "Surely this will not work?" She knew what she was doing and truly, made it so.

He read on: "I had to have him piped to the flight-deck as this was all or nothing. I knew as soon as he walked down the Port Waist towards me... I just knew! Not sure what has happened to me, but it feels right to feel like this at last!"

She wrote beautifully about their time at the hotel after the drive to Sliema and his heart jumped when he read about their first parting when the affair was about to get real. She had written, "Goodness, my juices burst when he put his hand on my neck and rubbed the downy patch of hair in front of my ear. He loved it. I loved it. How wonderfully different, erotic and exciting."

He flitted back and forth and on November 20th, another Saturday, he found a large professional black and white photograph of the two of them asleep.

Gideon had no idea how this had been taken. Clearly they had been making love and had fallen asleep. He was in an embryonic position and she was holding him like a child. Her chin was on the top of his head and her arms were around him. He was holding one of her hands. He was not emotionally ready to take in this image as he had never seen it before.

She had written on the page for that day, "M gave us her room with its magnificent view as she was staying overnight with Woody, who was on stand-by because of a Russian Whiskey-Long-Bin which had surfaced somewhere off Sardinia. The most wonderful night with the Boy. He fell asleep straight away and I cried for his soul. I cannot ever leave him to this beastly world alone."

She had clearly slid the erotic image into the diary at that page for a reason.

He remembered now. M was Melanie and she was a budding Wren photographer. She had been an Air Mechanic and was then selected to be trained as a darkroom assistant, which led to full integration and parity with the Naval Airmen Photographers. This is where she met Woody. Melanie had been drafted out to HMS St Angelo, attached to the RAF station at Luqa and she had the facilities to develop any images as she was part of the hush-hush underground band of people reporting on Soviet movements in the Mediterranean.

Melanie had written on the back of the photograph, "Darling! Woody called away to fly so came home to drop my gear off and could not resist how magical you looked as you lay there together. You nearly made me cry to see you there as one. How many people find that? Love to you both." It was signed, 'Mel' with four kisses.

When he came to the end, Gideon reread some parts, darting all over the place. He could not understand some of her references, though he had studied Greek mythology over the years, and some parts were written as poetic prose, which was so very her.

He clearly was the first man she had ever been close to. She had written passionately about him and even after everything, he hadn't realised quite how deeply she had felt about him.

He loved all the secret coded sobriquets she had used. Some he could work out and some were a total mystery. He was B for obvious reasons and Mickey was WJ for 'Windjammer,' which was a robust merchant sailing ship or a weather-beaten, crusty old sailor! Mickey would have loved that. M was Melanie and W was Woody.

He read again the part where she took him for that second drink. It was full of joy about meeting him alone and the final sentence pushed painfully on his heart. He read it aloud, alone on the beach. "Gideon! For me, everything begins today."

The last day they were together was a Sunday and on the Monday page she had written, "I know he really loves me. That's all that matters to me."

Chapter Forty-Three

Aeolus still whispers

Her diary included another small black and white photograph that he had never seen before. It showed the two of them in Tower Road in Sliema: Gideon was sitting a wall with his arms around Xanthe and she was standing in front of him facing the camera with her arms wrapped around his. He remembered that a local taxi driver had taken the picture for them. Gideon's heart clenched at the distinctive atmosphere that seemed to surround them. On the back was a lemniscate, that figure-of-eight on its side meaning infinity, and four kisses.

When you look at old images of lovers all over the world – lovers going off to war, lovers returned and gazing into each other's eyes again – you have a sense of what they were thinking and feeling. These were such images, and those thoughts and feelings came flooding back to Gideon.

He wanted to pay the ferryman and be with her forever. He wanted the wind to atomise him and take him be back to be with her amongst her gods.

He stood there on the shore and tore out the pages of her diary one by one, then watched those flimsy pieces of paper dance in the wind before falling into the sea. He had to do it. She would have approved, he was sure.

"S'agapo," he said to the sky and as he kissed the wind that kissed her soul.

He remained entranced until he had the hotel bar in sight. His heart was in a constant state of ataraxia because she had been there in that moment when Aeolus had whistled to him that everything was as it should be. Life moves on.

Yes, Gideon thought, he would have given up all his experiences and travels to have her as his life-long partner. Though in a strange way, she had been. This had been his perfect moment: the whole five months with her, and it could not be recaptured however hard he tried. And why should he ever want to better these memories?

Gideon arrived at the breakfast room the next morning and spotted Jess looking at a menu. He walked up to her and sat down.

"Have you informed the receptionist?" she said, searching his face. "Has your Aeolus given you some closure at least?"

"Well," he said, "I think I have an ending for my story. Athena the goddess of wisdom came down to Earth to seduce this ordinary boy. She knew she would find him and that he would love her back."

"And she'll keep him forever?" asked Jessica.

"Indeed," said Gideon with kindness in his eyes.

"Lucky girl. Call me if she lets you go, please?" she said with a smile, handing him her business card.

Fate. The evolution and progress of events outside of anyone's control, predetermined by some unseen force or maybe, just maybe, the goddesses of Ancient Greek mythology controlling the outcome of a coin toss?

Later, Gideon stood on the veranda of the hotel bar and thought of Epicurus and his philosophy. "Death does not concern us, because as long as we exist, death is not here," he had said. "And when it does come, we no longer exist." And yet, the Greeks' images and stories of all their gods and the Elysian fields were enchanting to them, and to Gideon too.

And Gideon was an empiricist too. Xanthe had taught him to believe that the senses are the only reliable source of knowledge about the world. He looked at his watch and it read 1832. Who would not believe that she was there all around him at that precious moment in time?

Time for a sundowner, then? Time for a JC. Gideon's heart soared but when he looked at his watch again, the minute hand had clicked on and it wasn't 1832 anymore. The time had passed. Tears were running down his face. He imagined them evaporating, ephemeral, and he reached out to grab what was not there before the breeze whisked it away. But he was at peace now, wasn't he? He was complete and ready to move on. Home is where your heart is, and here he was at home.

The wind blew and he thought he heard the cadence of her voice? But no, it was Aeolus softly whispering that she loved him.

.